Space Ark

by

Thomas Hubschman

Saga SF

2002

Space Ark

Cover by Eric and Isaac Black

Published by
Saga SF
473 17th St. #6
Brooklyn, NY 11215-6226

http://savvypress.com/sagasf/index.html
Email sagasf@savvypress.com
Fax: 1-443-238-0770

Printed in the United States of America

ISBN 0-9669877-5-6
LCCN 2002092334

Chapter One

Morning sunlight streamed in through the big, cathedral windows. Twenty mental retards were at play on the smooth, polished floor. Some were laying wood blocks end to end. I watched one, a bald middle-aged imbecile with tufts of gray hair sprouting just above his earlobes, and thought that, given a perpetual supply of those faceless cubes, he would lay them from here to the end of the universe and back, forming a great, perfect ellipse. His concentration was complete, his determination unshakable. Each day he performed the same ritual—or was it actually an infantile experiment? Only the attendant, a bruiser well over six feet, could break his fascination, and not without a fight.

It was mid-morning. Playtime would continue for another hour. I looked out through the clear polysilicate wall. It was full spring on Earth. When I last left my home planet, it was deep in the grip of a northern winter, the capital of the New Worlds Confederacy blanketed beneath ten inches of snow. The big outer-planet shuttles were being diverted to landing fields further south. The President was vacationing in Jamaica.

Since my return I had spent a good part of my time watching the small buds of a sycamore tree slowly open. Imprisoned as I was, I became a connoisseur of the crocus and the hyacinth. What else could I do? Branded as mentally defective by a government I had spent ten years serving—for the most part in capacities such as Waste Control Inspector for the Jovan moon system—now I was condemned to spend the rest of my days in a state hospital. Was this the thanks I got for my long years of service, not to mention the final, nearly fatal mission that ultimately landed me in this sorry mess?

As I scanned a clump of lilacs near the small park adjoining the hospital grounds, I realized what a mistake I had made in reporting my fateful discovery directly to a politician. I should have gone first to my immediate superior in the Division for Colonial Affairs, let him spring it on his own boss, and him on his, until word reached the President through ordinary official channels. That way I would have spared myself the humiliation of being diagnosed a fool (how could I know my speech would sound like gobbledygook after several days of hyperphotic travel?) and perhaps have saved the solar system as well from a cataclysmic fate. The President might be able to silence one junior-grade civil servant, but he could hardly keep under wraps a piece of news an entire governmental department had been exposed to.

Marshall Lynch had been a boyhood hero of mine, along with millions of other youths. He was also my ultimate superior as President of the New Worlds Confederacy. I would have laughed at, then probably slugged, anyone who maligned the man, until the day he had me thrown into this booby hatch for telling him that the end of the world, our entire solar system, was at hand.

The gray-haired moron had reached the wall and was beginning a second line of blocks, keeping them strictly parallel with the first. Drool had accumulated on his bottom lip. His baggy pants were half off. He looked like any two-year-old cutting a back molar. Only the regularity of the lines he was constructing suggested a more mature, however twisted, intelligence.

He never invited me to join his game. But he seemed to know I took a special interest in it. When his daily project approached my usual post near the window, his eye would catch my own and a flicker of something—was it cunning?—came alive there. In his childish mind perhaps he saw me as an accom-

4

plice. He might even be hoping to make me his playmate, as others had tried to do when I was first placed on the ward. A gang of retarded adults can be every bit as impetuous as the infants they emulate. It was boredom with my unfertile adult imagination that finally caused them to leave me in peace. If I had had to defend myself from their collective will, I would have been mincemeat by now.

I sized him up for a possible confrontation. Unlike most of his mental contemporaries, he was a lightweight. I could take him with one hand behind my back.

His line, until now strictly parallel to the one already stretching from one end of the ward to the other, veered off radically as it came near where I was standing. He added more blocks in a seemingly haphazard way, causing the line to zig and zag. I watched, wondering if something in his brain had gone haywire.

The pattern now stretched almost to the window. For a moment I thought he would continue on until the thick polysilicate wall stopped him. But then the line of blocks abruptly came to a halt and, after a quick furtive look over his shoulder he returned to the middle of the pattern. Hurriedly, he extended the lines between two points of the zigzag, forming an imperfect parallelogram. Then he added several blocks to one corner of the figure, making a small triangle.

If you mentally erased the blocks between the points of the pattern, the figure looked like a molecular diagram or even a constellation. First I tried to fit it into the shape of an atomic structure. It came close to the configuration of some carbonates I once had to sketch for a chemistry class, but it was too loose a pattern to make anything definite out of it.

Next I matched it with the constellations visible from the northern hemisphere. Here I was on more familiar territory. I was no astronomer, but any spacedog knows the constellations. Stars are to him what channels and sandbars are to a river pilot.

5

I started with Ursa Major and worked my way south. None of them quite fit.

I continued across the ecliptic into the southern hemisphere. The game was getting tedious. I didn't really expect to find a set of stars to match the imbecile's block figure. Still, did I have anything better to do? Sadly, this was the best mental stimulation I had had for several days.

I worked my way to the Southern Cross without success. I was running out of stars. It was almost snack time and, childish as it seemed, I looked forward to my cookies and milk as much as any of my impaired brethren. But thanks to my long years of academic training, I was also determined to solve the conundrum on the floor in front of me. I passed quickly through Libra and Scorpius, heading towards Ophiuchus at the very tip of the southern hemisphere. Then something made me pause and retrace my route in the direction of the Southern Cross. Was I mistaken, or did that lopsided parallelogram and the triangular cluster of blocks at one of its points look like...?

I moved to one side to better orient myself to the northern end of the constellation. Imagine my amazement when I saw that it fit perfectly. There on the floor beneath me, made of plastic children's blocks, was Centaurus—the very star system I had just escaped from by the bare skin of my teeth!

The man watched my reaction with that look of cunning I had observed earlier. Only this time there was added an undeniable and mature intelligence. I started to say something, but the finger he placed across his lips reminded me that we were being watched. I heard the attendant's heavy tread approaching. My astronomical friend began rearranging his blocks. I pretended an interest in a group of starlings on the lawn outside. The attendant came to a halt just a few feet away from us. My friend continued moving his blocks about as if trying to form a new pattern. Unable to produce the figure he wanted, he pushed them all together and began again. More drool issued from his bottom lip. The hair on the back of my head, like so many ten-tacles, sensed the attendant's powerful presence behind me. Thus far he had left me alone, perhaps under orders. But from the way I had seen him manhandle some of the other "patients," he didn't seem like the sort who enjoyed leaving anyone unmolested.

Unsuccessful a second time, the balding man suddenly began to throw a temper tantrum. I had seen a number of such outbursts in the past week. I hardly paid them any attention anymore, except to put plenty of distance between myself and the one acting out. But this was no ordinary tantrum. The imbecilic figure kicking his feet in the air and screaming at the top of his lungs was not just a more intriguing version of the other retards. He was play-acting, and doing a good job of it, I noted as I jumped aside so as not to catch one of his kicks.

But whatever differences I myself had noted between this man and the other patients, the attendant saw merely another opportunity to exercise his sadistic bent for keeping order. With one swat of his meaty hand he sent the man flying across the shiny floor, only coming to rest after slamming into one of the thick polysilicate windows and bouncing back half a dozen feet toward the attendant. The brute reached down and picked him up by the scruff of the neck with little more effort than a mother cat might pick up a kitten, and dragged him to the Quiet Room at the end of the ward.

When the attendant returned a few minutes later, he eyed me carefully before dealing with some of the other patients who were also acting out. I noticed that when one threw a tantrum a number of others would behave the same way shortly afterward. But these strictly sympathetic outbursts were easily controlled. A slap or two administered here and there, and everyone was back to playing blocks and paper dolls.

I waited anxiously for the time when my new friend would

be released from the Quiet Room. Up to now I had made it a point to show that I was not like the others. My speech, impaired by my experience on Alpha-II and by my dash home to warn Earth of the impending disaster threatening the solar system, seemed to be returning to normal. I was eager to try speaking again with an adult—and preferably not the heavy-handed attendant.

The man was released the next day and returned to the ward. He wore a big pout and an ugly bruise as the attendant dragged him across the floor and deposited him next to a group of younger patients playing peekaboo. They paid him no mind as he sat making faces at his feet like any sulking child. His performance was so good, in fact, that I wondered if I had been mistaken earlier. Maybe the pattern he had made with those blocks was just the product of chance. There were scores of constellations visible from Earth. The odds of putting one together haphazardly were perhaps not so great. But why Centaurus? And why that particular look of cunning? No, taken as a whole, the episode was too pregnant with possibility.

My problem was to find a way to communicate with him without letting the attendant know what we were up to. That would be more difficult than it might at first seem. I was pretty certain that I was under some kind of surveillance, despite the diagnosis of imbecility that had accompanied me to the hospital. If my friend was also mentally sound, then he had also been misdiagnosed or had been placed here for entirely non-medical reasons. I still had no notion that anyone could be kept in an institution against his will for "political" reasons. I half-believed that my own confinement was some kind of mistake. But my education in this respect was about to take a great leap forward.

I found my opportunity that night. The night attendant was much more lackadaisical than his daytime counterpart, though hardly less sadistic. If he found someone awake after lights out, he used a thick leather strap to ensure that order, as he perceived it, was restored. But after a while, around midnight, he usually dozed off. During my first couple days on the ward, when I still believed that some honest mistake had been made in my case, I tried to reason with the staff. I was more concerned with getting my message out to the scientific community than with regaining my freedom, much as I longed for it. But I might have saved my breath. Whatever the condition of the patients themselves, the mental state of the staff was even more hopeless. They scarcely seemed human. Their eyes showed little trace of intelligence and they seemed incapable of understanding even the simplest idea.

I waited till I heard the long snores of the night attendant at the far end of the ward. Then I cautiously slipped out from under my bedclothes and tiptoed toward the bed the baldheaded man was occupying.

My feet scarcely made any noise on the hard, highly polished floor. But my knees were trembling at the thought of being found out by the attendant and his thick leather strap. I didn't think myself a coward, but I had witnessed that strap in action a couple times in the past week. There may be more sophisticated means of working one's will on another, but I doubt that many left welts the size that strap did.

I stopped breathing when the attendant's snores ceased abruptly and the cot creaked under the weight of his shifting body. White moonlight was pouring in through the big arched windows. On the lawn outside a doe and her fawn were nibbling at something in the grass, visitors from the dense forest that surrounded the hospital on three sides. The doe raised her head and listened, as if she too feared the night attendant. Then the cot creaked again, the man gave a great sigh and his snoring resumed. The doe resumed feeding.

I tiptoed closer to the man's bedside. The other patients were all sleeping, for the most part peacefully. Only one was stirring, probably from a dream he was having. I prayed that his dream would soon end. I would have a bit of explaining to do if the attendant caught me confabbing with another patient at this time of night.

I finally reached the man's bedside and gently touched his shoulder. He started, turned over and squinted up at me in the moonlight. Happily, he did not cry out.

"It's me," I whispered. But how would he know who "me" was, unless he had a better view of my face than I did of his. So I identified myself by the figure he had made for me on the floor that morning. "Centaurus."

He immediately drew himself up on one arm and placed the other on my shoulder.

"I knew you'd respond," he said, studying my face with great intensity. Even in the dim light, his bright blue eyes shone with a keen intelligence. This man was no more related to the drooling imbecile I had earlier confronted than I was to a chimpanzee. "We have a lot to talk about."

We did indeed. Our only problem was how to do so without being discovered. So, before going any further he showed me how to make a convincing image of myself out of some pillows and a rubber ball, which he arranged beneath the covers on my bed. Then we returned to his bedside, which I agreed to hide beneath if the attendant made a bed check.

"I'm Boston Common," he said. "That's not my real name," he added. "It's just as well you don't know my real name in case you're interrogated."

"Why would I be interrogated? I don't have any information I haven't already given freely."

"I know," he said. "I know more about you than you realize, especially why you're here."

"In that case, I'd appreciate your sharing that information. All I know is, I had a temporary speech problem. And for that I got thrown into a mental hospital."

The attendant stirred again. We waited to see if he would

get up this time or merely turn over again and go back to sleep. A minute passed before we again heard his rhythmic snoring.

"Listen to me," Boston said. "We don't have much time. But you probably know that already. We know what's happening. Some of us do, anyway. Those who haven't buried their heads in the sand. We knew even before you returned from Alpha Centauri. But there was nothing we could do—not officially. We were fools even to approach the President with our knowledge."

"President Lynch knows?"

"Of course he knows."

"Then, why did he put me here? I personally took readings in the Centaurian system. I saw what the first shock waves were doing to Alpha-II."

"That's precisely why he didn't want you on the loose. Your speech difficulty was just a pretext. We had already warned him months ago."

I could scarcely believe what I was hearing. You must keep in mind that I had paid little attention to the politics of the New Worlds Confederacy. During the Civil War two decades earlier, like most boys I had idolized the Lynches on our own side and scorned those on the opposing side. Even the evidence I had found on Alpha-II of radiation warfare—banned by solar law for half a century—had caused me little concern. I had rationalized that, when the enemy was as cruel as the forces of the United Planets had been, any means to oppose them were justifiable. It would never have occurred to me that Marshall Lynch could have anything but the best welfare of his people in mind.

"But the President couldn't intend to just sit by while the solar system and everyone in it is destroyed," I said rather more forcefully than was prudent. Boston put his finger to his lips, reminding me of the gesture he had made earlier in the day. "The man is not an imbecile himself, is he?"

"Of course he isn't. Marshall Lynch is a shrewd, I'd almost

say brilliant, man if he weren't so blind to everything except his own self-interest. Even there, he suffers from tunnel vision.

"Listen to me, Walter," he said, using my real name and again laying his hand on my shoulder. "We have less than a month to organize an evacuation of the solar system."

"A month? Your calculations are off by three weeks at least. Even if the evacuation were to start this moment, we'd be lucky to save more than a few thousand people."

"Not so," he said. "This is still April. By our most recent calculations we have until early June before the first shock waves hit. Even after that we may have a week or two grace period."

"What are you talking about? In April I was still back on Alpha-II, trying to survive a mammoth hurricane...." I said, suddenly stopped by my own thought. "Unless...."

"Exactly," he said. "Time lag. I don't know what speeds you hit to get back here as fast as you did. But you obviously gained some time. Four or five weeks, I'd guess."

"I get to live those weeks over again?"

"All it means is that you arrived back on Earth a month earlier than you expected to. You probably didn't go through compensation. The only thing that matters now is that you, and a few others like us, are all this planet has left to get it out of the sorriest mess it's ever been in."

"What about the government?"

"There is no real government. Just a bunch of petty potentates who would sooner see this entire planetary system go up in smoke than lose the fat bank accounts they've spent their lives acquiring, mostly off someone else's sweat."

This sounded like sedition to me. But I had no alternative explanation for our leader's failure to act. He represented not just the states of Africa, Asia, Europe and the Americas. He was President of the entire solar system.

"What's your plan?" I said.

"First we have to get out of here. That's both easier and

12

more difficult than it seems. The staff here are all Cretins—literally. I don't know how much you spacedogs read the underground press, but these institutions have been run by such people ever since the end of the war."

"'Cretins'?"

"Man-made idiots. Surgical creations. Like the Simminoids."

"But the Simms are animals, animals with human hands, maybe sometimes with a voice box added. Even so, Simms were raised up from the purely animal level. But, if what you say is true, the people you're talking about were deliberately reduced to something less than human."

"In more ways than one. If you don't believe me, take a look at our keeper's brow the next time you get close to him. There's a surgical scar just behind his right temple."

How could a government lobotomize its own people? And how could it stand idly by while its entire population was destroyed by a supernova?

"What about them?" I said, indicating the beds nearby.

"Hard to say how many are man-made—'idiogents,' they're called. You can bet some are, though. Wasn't mental retardation cured a hundred years ago? Isn't that what they taught us?"

"This is awful."

"It's been a long time in coming. Some saw it even before the war. I was not among them, I'm sorry to say. I was like you, a regular babe in the woods. I learned my lesson late, and painfully," he said, touching his temple.

"You mean they…?"

"They did. Luckily, it didn't take. 'Even Homer nods.' Another week in this place, though, and I'll turn into an imbecile by osmosis. We have to get out of here, Walter. And we have to do it fast. So, listen up."

Chapter Two

This was his plan.

First we had to get out of the hospital. Like most large buildings, it was fueled by helium storage cells located beneath the big front lawn. The other sides of the building faced on the woods. We would escape at night, tap one of the cells for enough helium to lift a homemade dirigible and float to freedom over the treetops.

"What'll we make the balloon out of?" I asked.

Boston put his hand beneath the mattress of his bed and pulled out part of a plastic sheet.

"I have four of them. We can thank the stars we weren't put into a real jail. I might have had some trouble getting hold of so many in so short a time. Here it was easy. Every one of these beds has one."

"Still," I said, "it won't be as easy as that, will it."

I was hesitant for more than one reason: I still had hopes that the government would come to its senses, release me and begin a planet-wide evacuation.

"I've sewn these four together already. All I need is a fifth sheet—yours—and we'll be ready to go."

"How soon?"

"Tomorrow night."

"That soon?" "The longer we wait, the more chance there is the plan might not work. They might put us in different wards. Someone might discover the missing bedsheets. One of these dorks might pee in his bed, and there will be hell to pay if he did so on an unprotected mattress."

"What about the thing you sit in under the balloon?"

"The gondola. That stumped me for a while too. Then I realized that I was surrounded by potential building material," he said, indicating the play area on the other side of the ward.

"Toys?"

He nodded. "Blocks. Big ones. All we have to do is cement a few of them together. There's plenty of glue in the supply closet down the hall. It won't be the cushiest machine you ever rode in. But it'll do the trick."

"What if they catch us?"

Boston looked at me as if realizing for the first time just how leery I was about this venture. His blue eyes narrowed in the moonlight streaming in through the transparent walls.

"What's the alternative?" he said. "Wait here for doomsday? Or don't you believe our maximum leader is capable of letting that happen? Listen, Walt. This is April fifteenth. By May first there'll already be significant changes in the weather: windstorms, tidal waves, electrical disturbances. If Lynch and his boys had plans to do anything, don't you think they would have started to do so by now? And do you think he'd be letting you rot in this place in the meantime?

"Look," he went on, "I know you don't know me from Adam. I could be some malcontent or worse, as far as you're concerned. But think back a few weeks. Think back to what it was like on Alpha-II when the first shock waves hit."

"It was awful," I said, recalling the massive storm that almost did me in.

The next day he put aside the material he would use for the gondola. The balloon itself was already complete, right down to the guy lines which he had fashioned out of mattress stitching. At the end of the day's last play period he put the blocks he would use into a pile apart from the others.

We were ready. The day attendant handed over the ward to

his nighttime counterpart. The brute took a head count—using his fingers, of course—ordered everyone to bed, and lay down on his cot with a picture book.

We waited for midnight. The time seemed to pass in slow clicks. The sky was overcast—both good and bad for our escape plan. The extra darkness would help to cover our getaway, but the lack of stars to steer by might hamper us.

I looked into the gray clouds and thought about another sky I had left not so long ago. And about a woman—one of the small colony of orphans I had discovered on Alpha-II. They were all grown up by the time I found them, at least physically grown. They all subsequently perished in the hurricane, all except Sissy who fled from the others and returned with me to Earth.

What had become of her? Was she a prisoner like myself? Had some "patriotic" surgeon returned her to the infantile state in which I originally found her? Was that what they had in mind for me as well?

The thought that I might somehow be able to find her again braced me for the risky venture I was about to undertake. I missed her soft lips and silky hair. I missed our long nights of lovemaking.

Getting out of the building would be the hardest part. The ward was locked from the outside by a supervisor. The attendant was, in effect, locked in for the night with the rest of us. The emergency intercom could unseal the entrance. But that door was activated by the attendant's voiceprint. We would have to overpower him and force him to give the order that would open the door. Boston was wiry but small. That meant the job of restraining the attendant would be up to me.

Midnight finally arrived. Boston appeared beside my bed, and together we gathered the material we needed for the balloon. So far the attendant hadn't stirred.

Boston stashed the big blocks and plastic sheeting into a sack he had made out of a bedsheet. Then we tiptoed to the end of the ward. I slunk behind the sleeping attendant, locked his jaw shut with my forearm and dug my thumb into the critical nerve on his neck. His body heaved once in a powerful arc that almost wrenched him free. Then he subsided into unconsciousness.

"Now what?" I said. An unconscious attendant couldn't open the door for us.

"Wait and see."

A minute later the attendant started to come to. We sat him up so that his mouth was close to the intercom. He was already mumbling something about an escape. I forced his face closer to the wall.

"Escape!" he cried. I locked his jaw shut again and repeated my thumb-grinding operation. His body stiffened and then became still.

"Come on," Boston urged from the open doorway.

The coast was clear down to the main entrance where a lone security guard was on duty. With any luck, he would be asleep as well. He was, but not so deeply that I didn't feel obliged to give him the same treatment I had given the night attendant. Boston fished the laser key from his uniform and trained it on the main entrance. The big, polysilicate door slowly opened.

It was cold outside and damp. We were wearing just the thin hospital pants and tunics that all patients wore. The clouds overhead were broken here and there, but not enough to see stars through. Boston led the way down one of the more secluded paths toward the far end of the lawn.

"How do you know the valve's down here?" I said, jogging beside him.

"I saw them do a pressure check the day before you arrived. They added extra helium. If it's anything like the valves on the commercial tanks, it should be a cinch to open."

It wasn't. He sweated over it a good ten minutes without success. The hospital, meanwhile, was coming to life. Lights were going on all over. It looked like this would be as far we would get that night, or any night.

"Wait a minute," Boston said. "This looks like a test valve. If the tanks are full, and they should be, there should be an overload. If I can tap into that we'll have enough to get us airborne."

The test valve was operated manually. Boston connected the mouth of his balloon and turned it. At first nothing seemed to happen. Then the plastic sheets quivered. Boston gave a subdued version of a rebel yell and I hurriedly finished gluing together the building blocks.

"Are you sure this stuff will hold?"

"Don't worry. That's the same cement they use to join construction beams. Just don't get any on your hands."

Searchlights began raking the wide lawn and shrubbery. We ducked them as best we could, but by now there was no hiding the balloon which was billowing high above our heads.

"Is it almost ready?"

"Another minute," he said. "We can always let some gas out, but we can't let any more in once we're aloft."

Now there was shouting near the building. The security staff had finally come alive.

"It's ready," Boston announced.

We affixed the guy lines and climbed aboard the makeshift platform I had put together. Boston checked the entire apparatus once more, then reached down and cut the mooring line holding the big balloon to the ground.

Up we floated, soundlessly, without effort. Soon we were above the treetops, looking down at the shrinking figures running about on the ground below us. The only weapons guards were allowed to carry in a state institution were stun rays. But we were already out of their range. So, all they could do was shake their fists as we glided off over the treetops.

"What's to keep them from calling the police?" I said.

"By the time any police arrive we'll have landed and be safely underground."

He grinned and gave a tug on the starboard guy line. The balloon banked slightly, riding the stiff breeze nicely in a northerly direction.

"If this wind keeps up, we'll be doing better than twenty miles an hour. That should take us where we want to be in less than half an hour. Even the New Worlds Confederacy won't find us then."

I enjoyed the ride thoroughly, even though I expected a police sled to materialize out of the clouds at any moment.

"There it is," Boston said as we approached a small clearing in the woods.

"You don't expect to set it down there?"

But he did expect to, and did. In the process he came close to killing us both. A tall oak saved us at the last minute, grabbing hold of the balloon with its long branches and suspending us some ten or twelve feet off the ground.

"Could be worse," the pilot said.

After we dropped down from the gondola, we disentangled the balloon and buried it under the fallen leaves on the floor of the forest. Patrol sleds already hummed overhead, dropping flares and throwing shafts of light this way and that. Boston went on about his business like any scoutmaster on a hike.

Finally he was satisfied that the balloon was properly concealed.

"Follow me," he said.

Except for the occasional flare, it was pitch black in the woods. I followed him by listening to the sounds of his footsteps in the dead leaves. We hiked for a quarter mile or more, then he turned right and we continued for perhaps another half hour in that direction. It struck me that the man might just be mad. First that harebrained, albeit successful, escape from the mental hospital; now this blind trek through the woods with the police closing in overhead. Did he really think we could just walk out of this pickle?

I barked my shins on fallen trees and caught many an elastic branch in the face before we finally came to a halt again.

"This is it," he said.

"This is what?" I replied, seeing no difference between this particular part of the forest and the ones we had already passed through.

He squatted down and removed something from his pocket. By the dull light it emitted I could see it was a pocket transmitter, the kind children play with. Its range was probably less than half a mile. Who did he expect to contact with it, a friendly owl?

"Stand back," he said.

To my amazement, the ground began to shudder in front of us. A drone like that of a big, sluggish engine sounded. Then the earth literally opened up and a gaping black hole appeared.

"Follow me."

I climbed down some kind of rough staircase behind him. The earth closed again over our heads. We were immersed in total darkness.

We headed down some kind of tunnel, making what seemed totally arbitrary turns every so often. Finally we came to a halt and he took out his pocket transmitter again.

"Where are we?" I asked as he rapidly changed frequencies.

"You'll see soon enough."

Another engine groaned. The darkness parted, and a room appeared. At first it seemed no more than a dirt cellar. But as my eyes grew accustomed to the light, I saw that I was actually in someone's living quarters. All the comforts of home were there, a sink, a toilet, even a holovision which was tuned to a news program as we entered. It was only after I noticed these amenities that I spotted someone or something lounging in a dark corner. At Boston's urging I stepped into the chamber, and the earthen floor closed slowly behind me. I took a closer look at the creature in the corner. Sure enough, it was an ape.

Chapter Three

My experience with Simminoids was very limited. Since the first manus transplants were done, they had been taught to cook and sew as well as to do some of less skilled tasks such as picking fruit and tending to landscaping. Some of the smaller apes were famous for their way with children and were used regularly as nursemaids and babysitters. But communicating with them, even after giving them human hands and partly human brains, never got beyond the basic sign language that had first been introduced two hundred years ago.

They certainly hadn't advanced to the point that anyone thought seriously about admitting them to human intercourse. What, I asked myself, was this one doing lounging in an underground bunker, watching HV like any human and munching on what looked like dried fruit, probably heavily laced with bananas.

"Don't just stand there, Walter. Come over here."

I left my study of this enigmatic creature—did a smirk appear at the corner of its mouth or was I imagining things?—and approached a low table where Boston and a woman of about the same age as himself were seated. She was dark-skinned, gray-haired and quite attractive. She was also obviously glad to see him.

"This is Sheba," he said. "My wife."

"You mean, this is where you live?" I glanced again at the Simm on the couch. It was picking its teeth with a human fingernail.

"For the time being."

"You could say this is our summer home," Sheba said. "If we all live to see another summer," she added more seriously. "Sit down, Walter. I'll make you a cup of tea."

Boston watched me lower myself to the low, oriental table. We were both still dressed in the garb we had been obliged to wear in the hospital. He looked down at my tunic and laughed. "You look like a schoolboy."

"I feel like a damned fool in this outfit."

"I'll find you something more appropriate after you get some hot food in you. First, though, there's someone else I want you to meet."

He turned toward the Simminoid and said, "Rita? Would you come over here?"

The lanky ape—when she stood up, I saw why he had called her by a female name—got up, waited until the newscaster on the HV had delivered his punch line, then lumbered across the floor, her knuckles almost dragging on the hardened dirt.

"Rita, this is my friend Walter," Boston said, translating simultaneously into sign language. "Walter, I'd like you to meet a good friend of ours—Rita Ten."

"How do you do?" I signed.

She bared her teeth, then turned back to Boston.

"It's good to see you," she replied. "Was your trip successful?"

"Well, yes and no," he said without bothering to sign. Apparently, the Simm could understand spoken language without being able to reproduce it. "Actually, I spent the last half of my foray in a mental hospital. There was no way for me to contact you," he added, putting his arm around his wife. "In any case, it would only have alarmed you to know where I was."

Sheba got up to pour the boiling water.

"Sit down, Rita. There, beside Walter."

The Simminoid glanced at me cautiously, sensing my discomfort about her presence at a human table. She was, by all effects, an extremely intelligent member of her species. But she was still an ape as far as I could see. Nevertheless, I made a place for her.

"You see, Walt," Boston said, "I had also managed to schedule an interview with our illustrious President. Only, I didn't get as far as the Hexagonal Office. As soon as his chief henchmen heard what I was there for, they handed me over to the ISC and they deposited me in Bucks County Mental Hospital.

"I went to the Red House as a member of a delegation from all over the NWC. Simon Yoruba was with me, as well as Yevgeny Ping and Austin Black. Ping, by the way, is the grandson of the physicist. You remember him, don't you?"

"Of course," I said. I was not a scientist, but I knew who the author of the Regenerative Theory was.

"Well, we all were there, in good faith of course. Too good, as it turned out. We were all taken into custody. God knows what happened to Simon and the rest. They may have been idiogized by now. In any case, the mission was a total failure. Except that we finally managed to make Mr. Lynch show his true colors. I don't think anyone who knows what we know now—and suspected all along—has any doubts about that man's intentions. He'd sooner see us all perish than give up any of his power, or welsh on any of the bargains he must have struck with the powers-that-be."

"What can we do now?"

He turned toward the aromatic Simminoid on my right. "That's where Rita comes in."

The Simm regarded me again with caution. I suppose my attitude was written all across my face.

"I think our friend Walter," she signed, "is not yet willing to accept the idea of a Simminoid breaking bread or exchanging ideas freely with humans. Am I wrong?" she asked me directly.

I had no prejudice as such against Simminoids, as long as they did not pretend to be something they were not. One of my own nannies had been one, and I loved her almost as I would a human. Simms had become a common, indeed an essential part of our society, for small farmers like my father who owned three such creatures at one time, as much as for wealthy businessmen who employed them to cut their grass and shine their limousines. Unlike my present table companion, though, most of those Simms were shaved and clothed, absurd as the idea strikes me now. Until that night when I had to sit down at the same table with Rita Ten, I never gave the practice a second thought. A hairless Simminoid, radiologically depleted of his or her body hair and dressed up in overalls or even—pardon the expression— a monkey suit for those who acted as butlers and waiters, looked almost human. Some, who cultivated head hair and did not have features as emphatically simian as others, could indeed pass. Indeed, their behavior could set an example for some humans I have known. But no one, at least no one in my experience, had ever questioned what was their proper place in the social scheme.

"I know what you're thinking," Boston said after regarding me for a few seconds. "All I ask is that you try to keep an open mind."

I agreed to do so. Perhaps what bothered me most about Ms. Ten was not the fact that she was an ape. As I've already mentioned, I grew up in a household that was literally run by apes. I even played with their offspring, for a while not realizing there was any essential difference between them and me. Rita offended not by her species but by her arrogance, or by what I perceived at the time to be arrogance. I had never been this close to in unshaven ape except in a zoo. She was also naked, something as socially unacceptable as a naked human would be. And all that body hair also gave her a distinctly apelike odor. Most Simminoids used a deodorant when required to work indoors around humans. But Rita would need to douse her entire body with one to compensate for all that body hair. Everything considered, I needed not only an open mind but a new olfactory system, along with a new aesthetic, to accept her presence at that table.

"What is it we fear most from creatures such as Rita here?" Boston inquired.

"'Fear'? Why should we fear Simminoids?"

"Think about it, Walt. How much of our society is run by Simms? I don't mean mechanical things. I know that auto-brains and 'bots make the trains go and police our streets. I'm talking about jobs like caring for our young, sales clerks, farm labor, that kind of thing. Basic functions that require human-like intelligence and, even more important, feelings."

"What do feelings have do with it? I thought we were going to talk about the supernova."

"We are. Hold your horses."

I was beginning to feel uncomfortable, even angry. As a child of the New Worlds Confederacy I was taught how to be a good citizen of the solar republic. This meant abiding by the laws of its constitution and according every man and woman his full civil rights, as long as he and she remained productive members of society. It was a republic ruled by reason. Feelings or "emotions," to use the archaism my teachers employed on the rare occasions that they discussed the subject at all, only got in the way. Feelings clouded our intellect and numbed our will. They represented a chemical imbalance in the organism. A properly tuned body remained rational at all times. Our goal, though it was never stated as such, was to be as coolly reasonable as the auto-brains we depended on, even to the point of reading and writing and creating our so-called art for us.

"I'm afraid, Walter, that the Simms and all the other animals are our only hope now."

"You mean you're counting on dogs and cats to save us from the supernova?"

"It looks like we have no choice. Besides, don't be so quick to put down our furry brethren. A lot has been happening in the last ten years while you were out gallivanting about the universe."

"To make the Confederacy safe for the likes of you, don't forget."

He smiled and bowed his head.

"Touché, Waiter. I didn't mean to denigrate your work. I only meant that during that time you may have been somewhat out of touch with what was happening back on your home planet. Particularly what was happening among the Simminoids and even among the 'lower orders' of animals."

"Simms are Simms, and goldfish are goldfish."

Boston frowned and sat up straighter.

"To a point, yes. But it's not quite the way we were brought up to think. For instance, Rita here is not just the intellectual exception that you probably think her. There are thousands like her, just on this continent alone. But there's something even more important than the Simminoids' intelligence. It's their ability to communicate with other so-called animals. Forgive my use of the word, Rita," he said. "We still haven't come up with an adequate replacement."

The point he was making was valid enough. Simms were used regularly to herd cattle and generally keep domestic animals in line. They seemed to have a special knack for getting other animals to do what they wanted.

"Other animals respect Simms, Walt. There's a sympathy there that we humans have lost over the eons."

This was getting into pretty strange territory. Losing this sympathy with the lower animals, distinguishing ourselves from mere apes, was what made us specifically human, I had thought.

"How else can you explain the government's blind indifference to what was happening out there beyond Alpha Centauri?" he said. "Or why the good citizens of the New Worlds Confederacy, which looks more and more like the old one to me, are willing to follow it blindly down the path to their own destruction?

"We don't even know what fear is anymore, Walt. Like all other feelings, it's proscribed, verboten. Like all feelings, it impairs our ability to reason. We take pills to rid ourselves of it. We lobotomize ourselves the way people in other centuries had their tonsils removed. And the state doesn't even have to force it on us. We choose to do so freely. Free will, we were taught, devoid of any kind of passion, freely exercised, that's supposed to be man's highest state."

This was deep water for a simple geo-inspector. Still, if nothing else, what he was saying made me recall my experiences on Alpha-II. I had known fear there, and I was without any medication to dull the sensation. I had also known another feeling—a whole complex of feelings, really—because of Sissy. When I left Earth on what was supposed to be a fairly routine inspection of the Centaurian planets, I was still engaged to a girl from Kansas. After Sissy, I often wondered what that engagement was supposed to mean. Certainly my fiancée and I had never felt anything akin to the emotions Sissy awakened in me. Technically, it would have been a crime to do so, although like most citizens we were so heavily dosed with mood-controllers that it's a wonder we even decided to get married. It seems preposterous to me now, but when I left Earth on my mission to Centaurus, I had not exchanged a single passionate kiss with any woman.

"Could you be more specific," I said. "My head is starting to reel."

"It's simple, Walt. In every way that matters, Simms are human—the same as we are, I mean. Always have been. We were just too blind to notice. Too proud, I should say. The fact that now we can communicate with them verbally only emphasizes how intelligent they are. Other animals share this common nature, soul, whatever you want to call it. The Simms are just more humanoid. That's why we've recognized the quality in them first."

I recalled some experiments with rats that I conducted along with other students in my undergraduate psychology course. I also had had occasion to recall those rodents when I was lost in a maze of tunnels beneath an Alphanian mountain just a few weeks earlier. I hated to admit it, but I didn't behave much better than the rats had.

"Where does this all lead us?" I asked, trying keep up my skeptical tone.

"To the animals," he said. "To Rita here and the other Simminoids. But it won't stop there. The Simms, in turn, can tell the other domestic species what is happening and they, we hope, can even communicate with the birds and fish and other wild animals. By the way, some of them already have wind of a big disaster coming. There have been reports of tuna burrowing into the seabed, and the squirrels have gone underground, even though it's no longer winter and their usual habitation is trees."

I looked from Boston to Sheba and then to Rita, who was watching my reactions carefully. Was I surrounded by a pack of madmen, or were these the only sane inhabitants left on the planet?

"Boston," I said, "are you talking about a revolution? A revolution waged by animals?"

"Call it whatever you like. Call them whatever you like. All I know is, time is running out for this planet, and the only ones who aren't too stupid or too drugged to realize it are creatures like Rita.

"What do you say, Walter? Are you with us?"

Chapter Four

In the morning Boston and Sheba packed what few be-
longings they needed.

"Where to now?" I said.

"To a Council meeting."

"What council?" "The Council of Concerned Simminoids.
It's a clandestine organization. It's illegal, of course, for Simms
to hold a political meeting. So they wait for some big occasion,
like a political convention or a major sporting event, then take
the opportunity to get together without anyone but themselves
knowing about it."

"How long have they been holding such meetings?" I had
no idea that Simminoids did anything but attend to their basic
animal needs apart from the simple tasks they performed for us
humans.

"Quite a while. Longer than you'd think."

"How will we get there? The woods are probably crawling
with police and Confederacy agents."

"Trust me, Walter," he said, handing me a pair of pants and
a tunic.

"Try these on. They're big on me, so they should fit you.
We'll be traveling by public transportation once we leave here.
It's safer that way. You'll also need this," he added, tossing me a
wig.

"But this is for a woman's."

"The long hair will take a few years off you. Now, drop
your pants and bend over. I'm about to make you two shades

darker."

Pretty soon my complexion was so dark that I looked like I had just returned from Florida or the West Indies. Boston injected himself as well, with a double. The result in his case was a dark-skinned East Indian or Arab. The addition of a straight black toupee and a dye to color his beard the same color completed his transformation.

"Fortunately, I speak some Urdu," he said. "I just hope that, if anyone does question us, he isn't Pakistani himself."

"What about Rita?" I said. A hairy ape would stick out like a white cat in a coal bin.

My question answered itself a moment later. A very proper Simminoid, hairless, perfumed and dressed in appropriate Simm attire presented herself for our inspection.

"My God," I said. "Is this the same Simm?"

"It is."

I looked at the woman who had spoken, but she bore as little resemblance to the Sheba I had met the night before as her husband did to that drooling retard in the state hospital. She was now light-skinned, coifed in a long blonde wig and done up in a sexy outfit quite out of keeping with the conservative style she actually preferred.

"I spent half the night working on Rita," she said. "We depilated her entire body."

The Simm looked down with disgust at her bare arms. I understood now why she chose to live with her natural hair. Her bare skin had a flaccid, unhealthy look to it. Until then I had thought of that pasty, withered skin as the way a Simm looked naturally. I never gave any thought to the elaborate process that went into depilating each one of the natural hair follicles. It was as if Simms were born as hairless as human babies and remained that way throughout their lives—exactly the illusion we humans intended.

Rita knew how to play her role. She stood fairly upright, a

posture that would probably be giving her a backache before too long. Most Simms wore back supports to keep their carriage straight. Despite medical "advances" in that area, the Simminoid back persisted in sloping.

Otherwise she conformed in every detail to the way the servant of a well-off professional couple should look: standard Simm clothing, with falsies to indicate her sex as well as mimic the human form as much as possible, gloves to save any humans she might come in contact with from the offense of her touch, dark stockings to hide her naked legs and a pair of human shoes that must have been pure hell to wear.

And yet, despite these absurdities, she was dressed like millions of other Simms dressed every day. What was remarkable was that this was the first time I had realized what this involved.

We set off down a long tunnel in the opposite direction from the one by which we had entered.

"How long have you had this bunker?" I asked Boston, who was leading the way.

"It's not ours. It's Rita's. She's been a fugitive for over a year. There's a whole network of safe houses like this one. The Simms have ways of getting from one to the other, mostly through woodland. Of course, some of the Simms in the movement operate on the surface. In fact, many of the leaders are ordinary house servants. Naturally, they go about hairless and dress in regular Simms' clothing.

"Simms on the outside recruit other Simms and even make it possible for some of them to defect and go underground. It's similar to the way human slaves in various periods of history have helped each other. Of course, people like us are useful to them as well."

We had reached the end of the tunnel.

"This is the tricky part," he said. "Once we get to the station we'll be all right. The authorities will be looking for two light-skinned men and a dark woman. They won't be expecting a sexy blonde, an Indian and a playboy from Key West. Stay together and try to act natural. We'll take the monorail. We're only a few miles from downtown Philadelphia."

"You mean you're going right back under their noses?"

"It's the last place they'll expect to find us."

We came out of the tunnel inside a cellar of some kind. Somewhere above us I could hear muffled voices and the clinking of glass.

"Where are we?"

"Beneath a restaurant. There's a toilet just beyond that door over there. We'll go through it one by one, at intervals. Then we'll all sit down upstairs and eat a meal. Rita will eat in the Simms' section, of course. Afterward we'll walk out into the street just like any other citizens."

Sheba went first, Rita followed, then myself and, finally, Boston, to cover our back in case someone wandered into the cellar. It went without a hitch. Five minutes later the three of us were waiting for the maitre d' to find a table for us. Rita was already seated in the servants' section.

I ordered lamb. My hosts asked for vegetarian plates. It was only then that I realized how my eating meat would strike them. In fact, the idea had suddenly lost its appeal for me as well. When the food arrived, garnished with mint jelly, I could scarcely touch it.

"Eat," Boston said. "Three vegetarians might draw suspicion. The only good citizens of the NWC who turn up their noses at meat are the ones too poor to afford it."

"I can't," I said, irritated with him for causing my loss of appetite. I hadn't had a real meal in weeks.

"Then give it here," he said, dishing it onto his own plate.

I watched him chew with no apparent distaste. "How can you do it?" I said.

"The animal is already dead. Besides, the protoplasm of an

animal, human or otherwise, and that of a vegetable are really very similar. What I object to is not the eating of meat but the killing of a sentient creature to obtain it."

"Even so," I said, "I'm getting sick watching you."

"Two days ago you would have gladly gnawed on a horse if you could have gotten hold of one."

We took the magnetic monorail two stops to Penn Station, still an architectural wonder after three centuries. Our train was not scheduled to depart for almost an hour. I waited in the high-domed waiting hall while Boston and Sheba bought newspapers and magazines and sat down with something hot to drink in the cafe to read them. Rita waited with the other Simms.

Officials of the NWC milled about the concourse, on their ways to or from some bureaucratic business. I wondered if I would see my old boss from the Division of Colonial Affairs and if he would recognize me beneath my long hair and Florida tan. To further ensure that he wouldn't, I buried my head in a newspaper.

Of course, with the demise of literacy the very term "newspaper" had changed its meaning. The most sophisticated forms of print journalism were now just a series of photos copied from holovision newscasts, no different from the format of a wordless comic book.

As one of the few citizens capable of reading—I don't mean to suggest that it was banned; no one any longer wanted to read—the sight of all those great and semi-great people sitting and standing about, "reading" wordless picture books about world affairs now seemed to me ludicrous. My perspective, I realized, had changed. Before, I had thought it was I and my archaic hobby who was the strange one.

The train left on time. Like the commuter line we had taken to the station, it was a helium-lubricated magnetic that could make the run from Philly to Portland in just under three hours. From there you could make connections to all the major cities of the northern hemisphere via the arctic overland. If time was not of the essence and you preferred to fly, you could catch one of the big dirigibles out of Nova Scotia for just about any part of the globe.

We made the run to New York in half an hour. The train paused only briefly to let off tourists who still kept that ancient city alive long after it continued to have any commercial or social significance. Following the war, one of the numerous reclamation committees that sprang up raised enough funds to reconstruct the old Empire State Building. The idea caught on, and soon there were reclamation projects going on all over the site of the old city. By now there were a number of tourist attractions, little cities within the city, joined by a monorail built to ferry tourists from one locale to the next: Wall Street, Times Square, Rockefeller Center. A new project was started every year. There was even a residential area, a new New York, built within the old city limits to accommodate the growing number of workers and Simms needed to run the different attractions, complete with its own subway system and other urban facilities.

Our purpose for making the trip was ostensibly to attend the Inner Planet Regionals for the NWC Tennis Championships being held this year in the old Madison Square Garden—the sixth Garden since the original was constructed early in the 20th Century. Security would be tight but, for the most part, local. It would be another matter entirely when the finals were held in a couple of weeks and the great names of the Confederacy arrived to view them.

Of course, our real purpose had nothing to do with tennis. Since New York was a very old and largely abandoned city, there were lots of places to hold the kind of clandestine meeting Rita and her colleagues had in mind. We were counting on her to put us in touch with the Movement's leaders.

We went directly to a hotel and checked in, then set off on a tour of the old Times Square district. Rita accompanied us, sitting in the Simms' section at the rear of the trolley. We were allowed to roam freely about the arcades, peep shows and raucous neon signs, all faithfully reconstructed to emulate the Times Square of the late 20th Century. Only, the pimps and prostitutes loitering on corners and in dark alleyways were actually civil servants like myself, putting in their time toward a government pension.

Rita followed a few steps behind us. In reality, though, she was leading, and we took our cues from her. When she stopped at a reconstruction of an old movie theater—something called the "Paramount,"—we stopped as well, pretending it was our idea in the first place. She nodded at the ticket booth where a bored young woman made up like someone from 1950 sat yawning and filing her nails. Boston bought four tickets and we went inside.

The movie showing was a Western. I rather liked it, being partial to that genre. But we had scarcely seated ourselves in the balcony when Boston nudged me in the ribs and we began filing toward the rear of the theater where Rita was waiting for us. Without a word, she led us back toward the projection room, through a door and down a winding metal staircase. Soon we were in a basement again. Another door led us into a tunnel. We followed it in almost complete darkness for several hundred feet. At its end Rita paused, put her ear to the wall ahead of us and listened. Judging that the coast was clear, she knocked three times. Another door opened and we were admitted to some kind of meeting hall.

"Where are we?" I said.

"Beneath the old Garment Center," Rita signed. "It's due for a reconstruction of its own, but so far there's just a few excavations above ground. We're actually in the old buildings themselves. This was a meeting room for the board of directors of a major fashion company. I'm a bit of a history buff," she added with a Simian grin. "It pays to know your enemy."

We seated ourselves in some plush leather chairs and let Rita deal with the situation. A short Simminoid—hirsute, as Rita had been—gave us a suspicious look after he opened the door to Rita's secret knock. Humans were obviously not frequent guests at convocations such as this. Rita took him off to the side to discuss the situation.

"What do we do if the Simms want no part of us?" I said while we were waiting.

"We respect their wishes," Sheba replied. I took another look at the getup she was wearing and realized the doubtful impression she must have made on our host. She looked like anything but a human with a social consciousness about the servant class. "But I don't think they will reject us. Rita wouldn't have brought us here in the first place if she didn't trust us. And now that we're here, what would they do with us if they decided we weren't, after all, trustworthy? We have enough information to destroy the entire Movement. Besides," she added with a reassuring smile, "we are trustworthy."

Rita returned shortly with two other Simminoids. These obviously had been waiting for us and shook our hands warmly. They were both male, big fellows and entirely au naturel. I suspected that Rita would have shed her own slave clothes at this point except for the shame of her depilation. I had to admit that I felt sorry for her, a state of mind I had never before experienced toward a Simm.

"Welcome," the older-looking of the two Simms signed. "We badly need all the help we can get, especially from our human brothers. I call myself Mneh, an ape word for 'friend.'

"Sit down, please," he went on, sending the younger Simm away to prepare some refreshments.

"We meet none too soon," Mneh signed with the same kind of human hands that had been grafted onto Rita and most of the other Simms in the service of humans. These artificial limbs suddenly seemed very grotesque, although I had been living with human-handed Simms all of my life, the cloned limbs attached at an early stage of their lives to grow with them and so seem as "natural" as my own hands did to me. Only now did I see what an insult they constituted, an affront not only to their physical integrity but to their dignity as apes.

"Boston here advises us that we have less than a month to organize an evacuation. Of course, the NWC will oppose it, has already done so, in fact, jailing or lobotomizing everyone who has spoken up publicly for it. The situation isn't any better on the other planets. Being completely dependent on Earth for their vital technology, they have less chance of effecting an evacuation than we do.

"As Rita has no doubt pointed out, that leaves the job to us Simms and our furry brethren," he said. "We have already begun to communicate with the domestic animals. We can't expect the same kind of conscious response from them that we might get from a Simminoid or even," he said, "a human, on occasion. But we've made real progress. I think we will be able to count on them. Few humans," he added, looking my way, "can imagine how keen a sense of justice the average dog or cat has. Centuries of maltreatment—even torture under the guise of scientific experimentation—have left a kind of racial memory in them. They are actually more easily convinced of what is about to happen than are most Simms, who by now identify almost completely with their masters' interests. Even so, my own species will be adequately represented when the time comes."

With that, he sat back and sipped some tea. His dark, close-set eyes studied us without arrogance or hostility but with a keenness that was hard to accept from a Simm. I had known few humans who were capable of the kind of presentation he had just made. I was wondering how many more there were like him when, as if reading my thoughts, he signed, "No, Mr. Centaurus, I'm not a genetic freak. Simms such as myself have been around for well over a century. You didn't think you could graft human hands and parts of human brains into us without our eventually using these capacities in a human fashion? Not that we didn't lead an inner life before that which wasn't every bit as feeling and intelligent as your own, thank you. Each species, it seems, has a blind spot about the capacities of another. None of us wants to admit that we aren't at the top of what used to be called the evolutionary pyramid. Believe it or not, I once considered it belittling to address a human as an equal."

My eyebrows must have shot up because he smiled and said, "But, as you can see, I have grown democratic in my old age."

Chapter Five

Mneh said that it was not safe for the four of us to travel together, even in the underground railway. Rita would be all right on her own. Humans had trouble distinguishing even one of their own Simms from another. False identification papers would be provided for her and the brand on her forehead would be altered. She had covered the old brand with makeup and traced a new one on top of it. But that arrangement wouldn't be good enough if she were stopped by the police and interrogated.

Sheba would remain in the bunker until the last of our confederates had made their getaway. She would join Boston, myself and the Simms at the point of liftoff. Boston bid her goodbye with a tenderness I had never before witnessed. Without a continual ingestion of drugs to alter and re-alter his states of consciousness, he seemed remarkably at ease with his natural feelings. I was having considerably more difficulty myself. I had at some point known fear as well as love, anger, hate and all the other emotions. But until I was stranded on Alpha-II, I was never without a medication to modify these unwholesome humors. They were officially considered a kind of illness, symptoms of a primordial past which we were in the process of eradicating. Many had already succeeded in suppressing that residues of that past— or at least appeared that way—and were held up as examples for the rest of us. But most people still popped mood levelers as if they were candy.

Mneh led us through an underground passageway that must

have served as an arcade of some kind in the heyday of the old city. Some of the shops still displayed mannequins dressed in 21st-century clothing. I couldn't help smiling at the fashions of that time. It wasn't their archaic look that amused me so much as the resemblance they bore to the fashions of my parents' own generation—short-skirted tunics and wide, outrageously decorated hats. No one wore hats anymore.

The passageway ended at a subway station.

"This will be the hard part," Mneh told me and his other three traveling companions—Boston, the young male Simm who had accompanied him when he greeted us and a female. "The tunnel ahead is blocked. We'll have to go outside to reach our own underground terminal."

He led us up a complicated nexus of passageways, each leading to a staircase that brought us one level closer to the street. Finally I saw sunlight flooding down the staircase just ahead. Mneh reconnoitered to make sure no patrol craft were in the area. Then he motioned for us to follow him up.

We were on 42nd Street, just a few blocks from the Times Square restoration project. But we may as well have been on an asteroid. The tall buildings were in a long, slow process of decay. Some had already lost their facades. Rubble from the falling brick and mortar covered most of the street, which had caved in at several points.

And yet, looking up at the skyscrapers, some of which still stood proudly in the morning sunlight, I could see what this grand avenue must have looked like two centuries past when shoppers, businessmen and pretty secretaries thronged its sidewalks and petroleum-powered cars clogged its thoroughfare.

I had very little chance to stand and gawk, though. Mneh insisted that we keep up a brisk pace, keeping close to the buildings on the shadowed side of the street. When we reached Fifth Avenue, still distinguishable not just by the tangled street sign at the corner but by the grand view up and down the once-famous thoroughfare, my attention was drawn to a pile of stately rubble on the southwest corner. I asked Mneh what it was.

"This," he signed, pausing to contemplate the structure for a few seconds, "was once the heart of a great system of learning based solely on the printed word. People such as yourself could enter that building and find information on every conceivable subject, even on the intelligence of apes."

"What sort of place was it?"

"A book place," he signed. "The people of that century had a word for it. He signed the letters L-I-B-R-A-R-Y. The word was not unknown in modern times, of course. Only, over the centuries it had come to mean a depository for the chips on which the

memories of auto-brains were stored. When a brain needed access to any information stored there, it simply plugged into its "library" and retrieved what it was directed to find.

"You mean they actually stored books there?"

In our own day books, like fresh food, decayed in a matter of days. I assumed this had always been the case.

"Not books as we've known them," he said, squinting against the strong sunlight flooding the street. "In those days books lasted decades, sometimes centuries. The idea, in fact, was to make them last as long as possible."

How I wanted to get my hands on even a few volumes from that building! If what Mneh said was true, some of them must still be preserved. But there was no time to stop, so I made a promise to myself that we would not abandon this planet without saving at least some of those precious artifacts.

"Don't worry," Mneh said to me as we continued on our way. "We've already collected a sizable number of old books— some of them from that very building. We won't leave Earth empty-handed in that regard at least."

It only occurred to me then why I had been accepted into the movement with such a minimum of scrutiny. With all those

41

books to be scanned for the vital knowledge that a newly-transplanted civilization would require, people like myself, readers, would become a precious commodity. I had assumed it was my knowledge of the impending catastrophe that caused Boston and then the Simms to single me out for membership in their Movement. Actually, it was for my hobby they valued me, a skill I had acquired by mere chance, or so it seemed to me at the time.

We had reached Grand Central Terminal. The interior was almost completely decayed. The once-ornate ceiling I had seen in numerous holograms lay strewn about the immense concourse. The remnants of a huge silver-nitrate photograph, the head of a 21st-century woman ten yards wide, smiled down at us with eerie joie de vivre. Mneh picked his way through the rubble, taking us past ancient sweet shops and newspaper stands. A stack of magazines lay untouched, waiting for some long-dead commuters to read them. A newly-elected president of the old American republic grinned up from its front page, full of the exuberance of his victory.

"This leads to another subway system," Mneh said, leading the way down another flight of stairs.

At length we reached the underground platform. Water dripped from several places in the overhead. Much of the ceiling had caved in, but the rubble had been partially cleared away to make a clear path. A single subway car, vintage circa 2000 stood waiting on the tracks.

"Is this our transportation?"

Mneh regarded me with amusement. "Not modern enough for you? Believe me, electrified trains were one of the most dependable forms of transport two hundred years ago. With the proper upkeep they ran almost indefinitely."

A hydrogen motor substituted now for the old electric truck. Otherwise, the vehicle was pretty much as it must have been in the old days. I sat down on one of its contoured seats, a series of which stretched the entire length of the car on each side, and began studying the map on the wall. It showed the entire subway system for the city. For its time, that system was a remarkable engineering feat.

But as I traced with my finger the subway lines leading out of Grand Central Terminal, I was at a loss to explain how any one of them could get us further than the city limits.

The car started with a jerk. I looked across the antique carriage at my traveling companion, much as an ancient commuter must have perused his fellow passengers. The younger male Simm, named Delhi for his place of birth, had not spoken—signed— since we had set out except to compare notes with the female. She also was relatively young, certainly by comparison with Mneh. But it was hard to tell exactly what age she was. There was some gray in her fur, but she was agile and, for a Simm, not unattractive. She bared her teeth in a Simm smile as her eye caught mine. I bared my own back at her.

We rumbled along beneath the ancient city. The black walls of the tunnel snaked by us, undulating with a hypnotic rhythm. Every so often a subway station, empty and dark, appeared outside the car for a few seconds, then disappeared into the eternal night. The only light was cast by the headlights of the old car as it felt its way along the ancient tracks. What a burden friction had been for people who lived in the 20th century, I thought, recalling how easily our own magnetic trains moved. How much labor and money must have gone into the maintenance of a civilization that moved on wheels.

We reached yet another station. This one looked identical to the others we had passed, but this time we came to a stop just short of its platform.

"The tracks go outside at this point," Mneh said. "Follow me."

We got out of the car and began walking toward the station ahead. We climbed up from the tracks, then slipped through the turnstile entranceway. We were now several stories above ground.

Beneath us stretched the northern reaches of the old city. There was to see except rubble, the one exception being a nearby circular building that was completely hollow in the middle. In its day the structure itself must have been white, although now it was now reduced a to dirty gray.

"What's that?"

"Yankee Stadium," Boston said. "A sports arena."

"What kind of sport?"

"Baseball. A game something like our own fieldball. In fact, fieldball probably derives from it."

I looked down at the thousands of seats arranged in three tiers in a horseshoe shape. The structure looked every bit as large as the old Federation Stadium in Caracas. We had been taught that the Caracas dome was the first of its kind. I wondered how many other "firsts" of my world were actually duplications of something our ancestors had accomplished long ago.

We climbed down a rickety metal staircase to street level, then descended still further on concrete to another subterranean station. There we boarded another subway car and continued our journey.

When we finally reached our destination we were in the suburbs. Mneh led the way down a broad avenue the middle of which contained a pedestrian mall outfitted with the remains of benches that people must have once sat on to take the sun. Wild vegetation now overgrew everything. Tall buildings on either side of the avenue—residences, Boston told me—were covered with strange markings, some elaborately figured in faded primary colors. Here and there a name was discernible. It seemed an odd way to decorate a building.

We were to travel by leased private hovercraft the rest of the way. It seemed an oddly exposed link in the underground system, but Mneh explained that this was actually the safest method of travel at this point. Our ultimate destination was half an hour's flight from the megalopolis of Portland.

The Simms traveled in the luggage compartment from this point on. Boston drove. I kept an eye peeled for police. Luckily, the ones we saw were only interested in speeders and Boston was careful to stay well within the limit.

Before putting down, we scanned the sky from one end of the horizon to the other, then docked in an abandoned strip at the southern end of the Catskills mountains. We exited hastily and camouflaged the hovercraft. Then we entered the woods, trekked to another of those trap doors in the forest floor and followed a long passageway into the mountainside.

"This used to be a tourist attraction," Boston said as we entered an immense cavern. Scores of humans and Simminoids were at work on a huge vehicle there. The cavern's roof was easily a hundred feet high, and the spaceship rose to within ten feet of that height. I guessed that the cavern was at least three times as long as it was high.

"How many people do you figure the ship will hold?"

"About a thousand," he said. "People and animals."

"You're taking animals with you, besides Simms?"

"Certainly. They don't want to die anymore than we do. Besides, we'll need them to populate our new home, wherever that may be."

The actual destination of the evacuation effort had not yet been discussed, at least not in my presence. It would be well outside the Solar System, of course. But how far outside? And how could a passenger list the size of the one Boston was describing be fed during that kind of extended journey?

"There are about fifteen ships such as this under construction in different parts of the planet. Another twenty or thirty are being built in the colonies, mostly on Mars and Titan. We hope they'll all be finished in time. If not, we'll leave with what we've got. We'll lift off here as soon as this one is completed. If we wait until the very end, the same people who refuse now to take us seriously will be searching high and low for something to get

45

them off this doomed planet and won't hesitate to shoulder us aside. Of course, there's also the danger of earthquakes and cave-ins once the nova's shock waves start to hit."

"What's the ship made of?" I said, following him onto a gangplank leading up to the vehicle's first level. Meanwhile, Mneh went off with the two younger Simms to introduce them to other members of the Movement.

"Spare parts mostly. Wrecks, outmoded models from our grandfathers' days, all reinforced with polysilicate to withstand high stresses. They'll do five or six sol. Maybe better. Enough to outrun the nova if we get away in time."

A young woman was welding polysilicate sheets to the ship's exterior. Her long brown hair reminded me of Sissy's. It had been two weeks since I last saw Sissy, the day Lynch's Internal Security Police separated us, shipping me off to the mental hospital and dragging Sissy off to who-knew-where. The welder, thinking I had taken an interest in her for another reason, smiled.

Boston showed me the engine room, a gigantic complex taking up a quarter of the ship's space. More than anything, its immensity showed what kind of old battle wagons the ship was being cobbled from. The newest thrusters took up less than ten percent of the vehicles they powered. My government-issue space sled, though not designed for interstellar flight, had contained a single thruster with a supercharger fitted on. The entire apparatus comprised less than five percent of the vehicle's mass. It looked to me like this monster would need all the magnetic thrust it could muster to lift itself into space.

"There was an aviator once," Boston said as we climbed back down the construction ramp. "He set out to fly across the Atlantic in a single-seat combustion-engine craft. He had to carry so much fuel to make the flight that his critics said the vehicle would never get off the ground. But it did. And he made it to France," Boston assured me, putting an arm around my shoulder. "And we'll make it too."

Chapter Six

During my first few days in the cavern I was not given any specific assignment. Instead, I was introduced to the collection of books we would carry with us to our new home. They were still packed in crates that had been used to ferry them out of the old public depositories, such as the one we had seen in New York City.

My job was to unpack the books, select what was most relevant to our needs, and have the rest stored in the cavern on the off chance that we might someday return to our home planet. We would have been happy to take them all, but their weight was prohibitive.

I cracked open the first box and removed a couple volumes. The first was Fanny Hill, a memoir of some kind. But it was written in a variation of the language that I found hard to make out. I opened a second volume, A History of the West from 1870 to 1994. Beneath the title was a name. It took me awhile to understand that the name was that of the person who had composed the words in the book. No one in my day actually "wrote" a book. Our detective stories, science fiction, even "Westerns" about cowboys on Mars—were produced by the same machines that were responsible for printing and binding them. They were about as memorable as the paper they were printed on, although I had to confess a weakness for a particular series of Westerns. The idea of an individual, human author intrigued me beyond description.

I opened to the first chapter and began to read. For the rest of the day I was lost in the late 19th and 20th centuries. It shocked, then fascinated me to learn that our ancestors were no more adept at avoiding war than we had been. Nor did they seem less cruel, more honest or in any of the other virtues superior to the men and women of the 23rd century. I laughed at the pomposity with which the most primitive inventions were touted and shook my head at the machinations of their politicians. Where was the progress that my teachers had so often expounded on? In what way were we better than these people? We no longer believed in the simplistic theory of Relativity or the Darwinian explanation of biological development. But who was to say that our own theories would not be laughed at by some future Grade-19 geo-inspector—if we survived that long?

The next book I picked up was Barchester Towers, by someone named Trollope. At first I thought it was another history. Its language was also archaic, but not as much as incomprehensible as Fanny Hill. As I read on, I realized it was a story of some kind, though whether true or made-up I couldn't tell. After the first few pages I also didn't care. I was in thrall to the author's voice, a fascination all the more remarkable for the fact that he had been dead for four hundred years. He seemed to be sitting there in the cavern with me, leisurely telling his tale as if we were old friends. I had never experienced anything like it, at least not since my childhood bedtime stories. Certainly nothing I had read from my own time or seen on holovision had ever give me anything like the same feeling of intimacy. But who can feel close to an auto-brain? Or to the characters it creates?

I pawed through the crate with new eagerness, seizing upon one wonder after another that I carefully put aside to read at my leisure. How could I leave any of these precious volumes behind? I had come to realize the state of starvation we suffered from—not a physical starvation but a starvation of—I found the word I was looking for right there on the page in front of me—"soul." It appalled me to think that I had lived thirty years of my life in such a state of deprivation. And, were it not for a quaint hobby I had taken up merely to wile away the long, lonely hours of space, I might never even have realized what I had been missing.

I requested and was given permission to begin teaching some of the others how to read and write. At first there was resistance to the idea. It was imperative that the spacecraft be finished as soon as possible. But after explaining that I would conduct my classes after hours and purely on a voluntary basis, permission was finally granted.

One of my students was the dark-haired girl who had reminded me of Sissy. She was a biochemist from Vermont. She had suspected something was going wrong in our corner of the galaxy when she detected an unusual amount of radiation in the blood serum of certain wild animals she was studying. Her superiors, obviously acting under orders, told her to ignore it. Their attitude made no sense, but she met with recalcitrance so frequently, no matter whom she turned to, that she began to lapse into a state of depression. The strongest mood elevators only gave temporary relief. Then one day she expressed her frustration to her cook, a Simm who happened to be a member of the Movement. The Simm told her what the unusual radiation levels meant and asked if she would like to join the Movement. It was a risky thing for the Simm to do, not just for himself but for the Movement itself. Luckily, the biochemist jumped at the chance, and here she was, welding polysilicate instead of analyzing tissue samples.

"You can't imagine how surprised I was to hear a Simm talking about radiation levels," Garnet—that was her name—told me. "I no more paid attention to my Simm than I did to my dog or cat, except that I petted them. Of course, the Simm could perform fairly complicated tasks like cooking, and could communicate on a very basic level. But I took all that for granted, just as I assumed that my dog could express his eagerness or anger by barking. I learned a lot from that Simm. He's here now. In fact, he wants to learn to read and write too."

I hadn't thought about what it would be like to teach a Simm how to read. He couldn't speak as we did, and his sign language, though capable of sophisticated expression, bore little relationship to any verbal language. Still, if I was to accept them as equals I could hardly deny them the literacy I myself enjoyed.

The construction of the space ship went on day and night. I worked an evening shift, giving reading lessons both before and after working hours. The day shift came to me on their lunch break. I also began a diary. Whenever I went on extended missions, such as my fateful trip to Alpha Centauri, I kept a journal to amuse myself and make the time pass more quickly. But I never took it seriously. Now though, after reading a few history books, I came to see how distorted was the idea of the past that I and other members of my society had. And if the distant past had been twisted to fit the political interests of the moment, how much more so would be more recent history? If we were to start a new civilization somewhere, it seemed to me essential that someone keep an accurate record of the events which had brought about such a bold undertaking.

Garnet was my best pupil, or maybe she was just my favorite. I had not been with a woman for a month. Such periods of celibacy were common enough for spacedogs. But in the void of space, one is not constantly confronted with bewitching eyes and shapely calves except in one's imagination. Besides, there were always "medications" to alleviate the urgency. Now, though, I began to feel a strong desire for this bright, beautiful woman. Sissy had shown me how to feel desire unalloyed by chemical stimulants or by mood "regulators." I wanted to feel that desire again.

We made love between reading lessons. Garnet was not so

uninhibited as Sissy, who had not had contact with civilization for almost all of her twenty-two years, but she was every inch a warm and loving creature. We made love every chance we got, and when we weren't making love we read together from the crates of books that I breathed, ate and slept with when I wasn't helping to build the ship.

Soon it was ready. The cavern began to fill up with all kinds of animal life. Wild animals prowled about, mingling with people, Simms and domestic creatures. They didn't much like space rations, but if we were all to live in harmony, they couldn't very well be allowed to feed off each other. I had to evict a family of muskrats twice from my book crates.

Of course, we humans couldn't communicate directly with the squirrels and bears. That was left to the Simms and the Simms' delegates, the domestic animals. Dogs were the natural and most effective go-betweens. We had our share of fusses, but all in all it was amazing to see how well everyone got on.

When the last silicate plate was welded into place, Mneh called all the Simms and humans together on board the ship. Although the word "ark" had become the common name by which we referred to our vehicle, none of us knew the actual origin of the term. Like most of our other words, we used it simply because it seemed appropriate. An ark was a ship used to escape a general calamity. But then I discovered in my crates a worn volume which purported to be a very ancient history of the Earth. Indeed, it began with the words, "In the beginning God created the heavens and the earth." It went on to describe the creation of the first man and woman and then to trace their descendants down through the ages. Who this "God" was and how many of the other details in the book could be made to jibe with modern scientific thought was beyond me. But one passage seemed especially apt for our present undertaking. I gave it to Mneh, who did not need any reading lessons, since he had taught himself how to read. It was from this text that he addressed his human and Simian congregation just prior to lift-off.

"And it happened that a great darkness covered the earth. It rained for forty days and forty nights. All the earth was covered with water, except for Noah and his Ark....'"

Whatever that book had been in its own time, it provided us inhabitants of the twenty-third century with a very real description of our mission. A reverent silence hung over the gathering as Mneh closed the book. It lasted a few more seconds, then the ship's officers began calling for everyone to go below decks and prepare for departure.

Our biggest problem would be eluding the NWC. This would be done, I was told, by transmitting mock images of our ship, confusing the government monitors about our actual whereabouts. At best, the ploy could only gain us time. But time, we were hoping, would be all that we needed. If the Confederacy wanted to destroy us, it certainly could. But what advantage, we reasoned, would there be in annihilating a few thousand refugees who would soon be out of their hair anyway?

The mountainside exploded away from us, revealing a starry sky above. The ship's big engines pulsed through the labyrinth of its decks and passageways. Almost imperceptibly, the Ark lifted off, accelerating quickly as soon as it was clear of the jagged mountainside. Apart from G-force, there was no sense of motion unless you watched, as I was doing, the rapidly receding Earth.

Soon the entire eastern coast of North America was visible beneath us, then the breadth of the continent from ocean to ocean all the way from Maine to the slopes of Nevada where California had broken off so precipitously. Then we could see South America and, to the west, the glow of dawn breaking over mid-Pacific.

My throat constricted at this final sight of my home planet. I had lifted off in any number of vehicles and seen this sight any number of times. But this was my first farewell.

At fifty miles out a missile crossed our bow. It detonated well to the east of us, having homed in on one of our phantom images. Two more missiles were confused in the same way and exploded harmlessly.

At fifty thousand miles scanners on the moon bases picked us up and asked for identification. To be on the safe side, we sent out more phantom images, then told them who we were and what we were about. They ordered us to return to Earth. In reply, we pretended to be having trouble with our communications and asked Moon Base to send assistance, giving a false coordinate. By the time their ships arrived we would be well out of range.

When we switched on the news the next morning, the anchorman explained the flashes of light in the previous night's sky as ordinary target practice. This led him into an editorial on military preparedness and the necessity for the General Assembly's passing the new and even bigger military budget without further delay. Who it was that the NWC needed to defend itself against was not spelled out. Apparently, "unfriendly forces" waited somewhere in the ether to pounce on poor little Earth and its helpless colonies.

We sped away from the sun at full throttle. The Ark might have looked like an old tub when it was being slapped together, but its engine was state of the art. At twenty-four hours out we rendezvoused with nine other ships that had made their own escapes the same night we did. Two others, Boston told me, were missing. Four additional vessels were expected to join us from the colonies. One had already arrived from the Venusian orbiter. It was essential that we all remain together. Our relative differences of speed over an extended period of time could put us permanently out of touch. Besides, only some of those on board the Ark knew where we were actually headed. Even Boston claimed to be in the dark.

I kept busy making an inventory of the books we had taken. Garnet was allowed to assist me, since her reading had advanced beyond anyone else's. Her literacy skills weren't all that were advancing. Like most of the rest of us who had recently detoxified ourselves from various medications, she was reveling in the newness of her unfettered feelings. Romances were blossoming all over the ship. You could scarcely take a walk down any promenade deck without encountering at least one pair of lovers. I was enjoying our lovemaking, but for me it was less novel than it was for her. I had known this bliss on Alpha-II with my womanchild. Sissy continued to haunt my thoughts.

Chapter Seven

After a few days of sleeping, eating, working and recreating pretty much according to much the same schedule we had been keeping on Earth, the leadership called another meeting. Since most of us were expecting that our ultimate destination would be revealed at this gathering, we were eagerly looking forward to it. Our sister ships from the colonies had made contact with us by now. They would participate in the assembly via holovision.

A hall located amidships, capable of holding all the ship's passengers when extra seating was added, was prepared. Along with the others, I sat anxiously waiting for the news we had been anticipating ever since our liftoff from that mountainside. Where was our new home to be? What would our life there be like? Did it have one sun or two?

The auditorium buzzed with anticipation. Simms and humans alike were fidgeting like kids at a puppet show. Garnet clutched my hand tightly, alternately laughing and crying in a confusion of more feeling than she knew what to do with.

Finally Mneh and the other leaders of the Movement, both human and Simian, took their places on the stage. The audience quieted as Boston stepped to the podium. He looked about the assembly and smiled.

"Greetings," he said, nodding his head like a pleased school principal, "children of the Ark. "We are met here as free creatures, male and female, Simminoid and human. We are met here as equals, sharing a common ancestry and a common fate. We have lived together, eaten together and—unless my eyes have deceived me—slept together as well,"—laughter—"as one people, without distinction of species and with one common goal before us, the preservation of all the species of our planet."

Applause followed. Then a hush fell over the assembly.

"Without further ado, I give you the person who, more than any of the rest of us, has devoted himself unselfishly to the common good of all Earth dwellers. I give you—Mneh!"

It was several minutes before the enthusiasm died down. Throughout the lengthy standing ovation Mneh sat, his gray head nodding in recognition, his lips parted in a smile. Then his hand was raised for silence and the hall became quiet as space itself.

"Dear friends," he began, exaggerating his signing so that even those in the back could see. "My heart is filled with love for you and with joy. We have successfully escaped from a planet of injustice, cruelty and discrimination. Our true destiny still lies ahead, and our journey is just beginning. Our flight will last several months, perhaps longer." Groans followed, but even these were good-natured. "Like Noah and his fellow creatures, we are embarked on a journey to a destination still unknown to us. I wish I could tell you what that destination will be. But I cannot. The supernova is still acting in an unpredictable way. At this very moment its first shock waves are striking Earth."

The lights dimmed. An image was projected onto the holostage.

"These are transmissions we recorded from a newscast less than one hour ago."

A raging hurricane, very similar to the one I had encountered on Alpha-II, appeared. Images of an earthquake in South America followed. Then a typhoon, then several volcanic eruptions. Mass graves were being dug.

"True to form, the government continues to insist these phenomena are all naturally caused, that nothing cosmic is at fault. Meanwhile, I'm sure Marshall Lynch has himself already abandoned the planet. This is another reason for caution. Our journey will not end until we have safely set down on our new home planet and breathed its fresh air. I wish I could tell you when and where that touchdown will be. But I cannot.

"In the meantime, let us watch and wait. We have a long journey and, for so many species at once, this is a relatively small ship. I ask that you show each other the same consideration you yourself expect. As it says in the good book from which I read before lift-off, 'Thou shalt love thy neighbor as thyself.'

"I now turn the meeting over to your capable flight commander."

There was no news, after all. Disappointment showed in all our faces as Simms and humans left the hall. Still, there was no question at this point that we had done the right thing when we chose to flaunt the authority of the government by abandoning our home planet. We may not have known where we were heading, but the evidence on the holovision had shown us well enough what we were heading away from. No one aboard that ship wished that she or he were standing on terra firma instead of winging into the unknown still in one piece.

There was not enough work to keep us all occupied full-time. A small contingent kept the ship moving on course. The rest of us had most of our time to ourselves. I was one of the lucky ones. Cataloguing the library took less than two weeks, but there was enough reading material to last years. I did a land-office business as reading instructor. And when I wasn't teaching someone his or her ABC's, I was keeping track of the volumes I loaned out and playing sleuth when someone kept a book longer than he or she had agreed to. If I tired of these activities—and sometimes when I didn't—there was Garnet.

We held assemblies every ten days. There was little to discuss apart from the news from Earth. Soon even those newscasts would stop, not because the relays weren't still working properly but because the inhabitants of the planet would no longer be capable of sending a transmission. The havoc was horrible. But even as we watched we knew that, distant as we were now from where those terrible scenes were taking place, the end already may have come for them. No form of life could withstand the final shock waves from a supernova. They would extinguish Earth like a candle, and the rest of the solar system along with it.

The assemblies became more and more devoted to pep rallies and gripe sessions. Living quarters were starting to feel pretty close, and spirits had to be kept up. Mneh himself appeared at fewer and fewer of the meetings, leaving them for Boston to conduct.

It was at the second general meeting that Mneh announced the word Simminoid was to be dropped from usage, along with the word human. He pointed out that Simms had endured the term as a slave name, a stigma that went with their grafted human hands and brain parts. In the same way, "human" had been used to denote the superior, ruling race of humankind. Since we were all now equals, we should speak accordingly. Therefore he asked us all to refrain from using either term again.

At the time it seemed like a good idea. We were all already uncomfortable with the words and tried to avoid them whenever possible. Were it not for the events that followed that meeting, Mneh's modest proposal might have gone virtually unnoticed.

But it was then that he stopped attending our assemblies. No reason was given. We assumed that the management of the ship required his full attention. He continued to send us messages through Boston or one of his other assistants. I myself also assumed that our leader was busy with ship's business, until my duties as librarian eventually brought me into direct contact with him.

Among our stock of books were three Bibles—the name given to the ancient text where I had found the Noah story that so fascinated Mneh before lift-off. As soon as we were safely out of the solar system and came to have lots of free time on our hands, there was a sudden run on those books. Everyone—everyone at that point who had learned how to read—wanted to read for her- or himself the story of Noah and to see what other stories the book contained. It was then, when the books came suddenly into such demand, that I realized Mneh had not yet returned the copy I lent him before liftoff. I didn't immediately ask for it back, assuming that his position afforded him some privileges in this regard. But after a full month had passed and the waiting list had grown to sizable proportions, I decided that I had an obligation to the rest of the ship's passengers to ask for the book's return.

So, one "evening" when the ship's lights were dimmed and a canopy was drawn outside to shield us from the light of any nearby luminaries, I made the long trek to the other end of the ship where Mneh's quarters were located.

I found Boston already there. I had seen very little of him on a personal basis since we had left Earth. He greeted me warmly.

"Walter!" he said, standing up to pump my hand. "I haven't seen you in a dog's age."

We began exchanged pleasantries for a while, and then I asked if I might see Mneh about some book business.

"You've certainly taken those volumes to heart, Walt. I was just saying to Sheba the other day, 'That G-Inspector has turned into a regular bookworm.'"

"How is Sheba?" I asked. I had seen even less of her than I had of Boston.

"Fit as a fiddle. She hangs out up on 'B' deck. She'll be sorry she missed you this evening. Well, perhaps another time."

It was all very breezy and friendly, but somehow his words had an artificial ring. This was not the same man who had helped me escape from me the state mental hospital and convinced me that Simminoids should have the same rights as humans.

I asked if I might see Mneh.

"The Master," Boston replied, "is meditating."

"'Meditating'?"

"An archaic term. It means to think deeply about something. Holy men like the prophets used to mediate. It put them in touch with the divine."

The only reason I had any idea what he was talking about was because of my own readings of that Bible book. "Holy," "prophets" and "divine" would otherwise have been as foreign to my ear as was the word "meditate."

"Does he…meditate often?" I asked.

"Every day. And when he isn't meditating, he studies. Usually the Bible, but sometimes other things. He's a very great person, Walter. We're lucky to have him for our leader. He's preparing himself right now for a long meditation. He'll also be fasting. That's what the prophets did—prayed and fasted, sometimes for weeks on end."

"How long will Mneh's fast last?"

"He wants to do it for forty days. But the ship's business can't spare him for that amount of time. He'll probably settle for twenty."

"Twenty days without food?"

"With very little."

"What does he hope to accomplish?"

Boston hesitated, then leaned forward and dropped the tone of his voice. "That's what he wants to find out."

I didn't bother asking for the Bible back. Mneh's meditation still had an hour to go. I said I had to get back to the library.

When I returned to my quarters I flopped down on my bunk and tried to make sense of what was going on. I hadn't gotten very far when Garnet came in.

"Do you remember," I said, "any passages in the Bible when one of the prophets goes away by himself for a while to fast and pray?"

"Didn't someone go into a desert for forty days and forty nights?"

"What did he do after he came out?"

"He lead the Israelites somewhere? Into or out of someplace. When he was in the desert he spoke with someone who told him what he should do, someone with a strange name. Jeh...."

"Jehovah."

"That's right. The Hebrew deity, the supreme being who was supposed to be responsible for the creation of the universe. He took a special interest in the Israelites. It doesn't make any sense to me."

"Maybe so. But it does offer an explanation for some of the things that have been going on around here."

Chapter Eight

I had other things on my mind besides Mneh's religious conversion. Marshall Lynch's warships had drawn to within tracking distance of our fleet. It seemed unlikely that he might still have any evil designs on us now that the destruction of Earth was an accomplished fact. If he did, we were not outfitted for battle, even a defensive battle. All we could do was keep him under surveillance and hope for the best. But even with his lighter, faster ships, he was still several days behind us.

Meanwhile, the fleet regrouped into a pattern that made communications as well as shuttling between the great ships easier. One of the first products of our improved intercourse with each other was the publication of the passenger lists for each of the vessels in the fleet. I scanned the thousands of names eagerly in hopes of finding Sissy's among them. Alongside the lists were posted private messages in auto-brain language from hundreds of passengers hoping to make contact with relatives and loved ones. Alongside these appeals were pictures copied from the ships' holovisions. I had to go through hundreds of tiny photos, hoping to find one of Sissy. Each day I made the pilgrimage to the central bulletin board. Each day I returned to my quarters disappointed.

Garnet noticed my depression and asked me about it. "Are you hoping to find one of your family?"

"A friend," I said. "A good friend. The woman I brought back with me from Alpha-II."

"I remember," she replied, eyeing me warily. "'Sissy', wasn't it? She must have been a pretty special 'friend'."

I glanced across the room where she was making out withdrawal cards for books. Her expression was deadpan, but there was an uncommon flush to her complexion.

"I'd just feel a lot more at ease if I knew that she'd gotten away safely."

"Unlikely, isn't it? Didn't you tell me she was picked up by Lynch's men at the same time they put you in that awful hospital?"

"Yes," I said. "I suppose you're right."

She finished the stack of cards she was working on, then arranged them into a neat pile on top of her desk. She got up, undid her tunic and let it slip from her bare shoulders. Then she walked slowly over to my bunk did her best to make me forget about Sissy.

At the next assembly we were told that Marshall Lynch's fleet was now less than two days' behind our own. Even accounting for a time warp, he was drawing dangerously close. Someone asked what preparations we had taken for a confrontation with the President of the New Worlds Confederacy—a constituency now reduced to several molten heaps circling a very unsettled star.

"Essentially, nothing," Boston said. Mneh, presumably, was "meditating." "If Lynch wants to cause trouble there's not much we can do about it. We certainly don't have the wherewithal to oppose him or even to properly defend ourselves. Apart from pure cussedness, though, what reason could he have to attack us? We certainly present no threat to his security. And we may well be the only other human beings he will ever again set eyes on. At this point, I would guess that he's content just to keep us on his scanners. He probably thinks we're on our way to a nice little planet to start a new civilization. If he can follow us there, let us land and then come in and take over, he'll be right back where he started—in the driver's seat."

"And we'll be right back where we started," someone quipped from the back of the packed assembly hall.

"I'm well aware of that," Boston replied. "But that is one contingency I can assure you we are prepared for—about as well prepared as we can be, given our circumstances. I'd like to say more, but I don't dare at the moment. On the other hand, if Lynch does decide to zap us, nothing else will matter anyway, will it?" he concluded with a wry smile.

The group didn't like the sound of that, but we all had too much faith in Boston, Mneh and our other leaders to press them on this point. If they said they had a plan to get us to our destination safely, we were willing to accept it, for now, on their say so.

Another week passed. Lynch dogged our tail, staying just inside the same warp we were traveling in. He could have closed at any time he wanted to and worked his will on us. But he continued to hang back, waiting for us to make the first move.

Mneh was into the tenth day of his fast. Apart from a brief appearance to his immediate circle just before his ordeal began, he had remained secluded. Boston was running the ship. No one had made an official announcement about the leader's prolonged meditation, but word spread soon enough on its own. It became the subject of jokes at first, then of curiosity and finally, as the days lengthened into weeks and he still had not come out of his seclusion, people began to wonder openly what was going on. Those who had, like myself, read the Bible probably had some inkling what he was up to, but even if you assumed that he was trying to emulate one of the Hebrew prophets, what good did that knowledge do you? Was he doing it out of some personal idiosyncrasy? Did he hope that somehow his prayer and fasting would protect us from Marshall Lynch? Or had the old ape just gone nuts?

Finally the twentieth day arrived. A special assembly was called. The hall was jammed for an hour before the meeting was scheduled to begin. As soon as I entered the hall and took my seat I saw that this was not going to be like any of the other meetings we had held. For one thing, the stage was decorated with purple bunting, giving it a somber, almost funereal appearance. Purple, I recalled from my reading, was the color of royalty. Was Mneh going to have himself crowned king?

Finally the time arrived for the leader to appear. But instead of a regally-clad ruler attended by an entourage of flamboyant lackeys and ministers of state, a stooped emaciated Simminoid, dressed literally in rags, his eyes watering copiously, his bent body supported by something that looked very much like a tree branch, shuffled out onto the stage. He stepped up to the podium, lifted his suddenly snow-white head and announced with exaggerated gesture: "I have spoken with the Lord!"

The assembly gaped incredulously at this apparition. A few tittered, but for the most part we were awestruck. You can't imagine what a strange figure Mneh seemed as he stood leaning on his staff, peering at us through leaky eyes.

"I have been to the mountain," he said, "and I have spoken with the Lord."

He spoke for the better part of an hour, no mean feat when you considered the shape he was in. But he never really got beyond the message summed up in his opening declaration. He had been to the mountain and "the Lord" had sent him back down to deliver his people out of the land of bondage. That was all well and good. As a matter of fact, whether sent by the Lord or not, he had in fact led us out of the sure death that had awaited us on Earth. I at least was able to recognize the biblical terms he was speaking in and put down his references to "bondage" and the like to poetic license. But what was all this rigmarole for? What was he leading up to?

He answered my question partially after he finished his description of his twenty days on the mountain. His bent form straightened and his eyes, by now grown fiery, stared over our heads as if at some image that he saw hovering above us.

"And I asked the Lord," he signed, still staring at that same spot as if the Lord were right there among us, "'Lord, what is Thy servant's name to be that shall accomplish all these things you speak of?' And the Lord said to me, 'Behold, thou art this same servant, Mneh. And henceforth thou shalt be known no longer by thy earthly name. From this day forth thy name is— Moses.'"

And so it came to pass that we got our very own Moses. He wasn't Hebrew. He wasn't even human. But he was all ours. And if we weren't a "chosen" people, who was?

The divine anointing of our leader had very little effect on the ship's day-to-day routine, at least not at first. It was almost two weeks before the first promulgation issued forth from Mneh's—Moses'—headquarters. And it was a disappointment.

It seemed the Lord, when he granted a private audience to our leader, had chosen to share a sumptuous feast with him. Mneh was understandably grateful for this in view of his weeks of fasting. But the food, like the Lord himself, was invisible to everyone except Mneh. He assured us afterward that it was a gourmet's delight—baked this and curried that—a description which did not win him too many friends among his space-rationed congregation. To add insult to injury, he asked us, in view of the Lord's own practice during the course of this feast, henceforth to eat only with our left hands. It did not seem much in the way of a divine injunction. At this point we were all inclined to consider the old Simm a bit balmy. But we humored him and went on eating as we always had—with the exception of a few natural left-handers who, half-jokingly, felt that Mneh's deity had indirectly put his seal of approval on them.

Meanwhile, Marshall Lynch continued to play cat-and-mouse with us. Some days he would drop back or even change course slightly, and we would hope that he had decided to light out on his own. But then he would tailgate us for a week, keeping us just within range of his drones. It was an uncomfortable way to live, but somehow we adjusted to it. Lynch became unavoidable, inevitable, and as such he relieved us of the responsibility of worrying about him. He took on the character of a natural calamity, like an earthquake. It may strike, and then again it might not. You didn't know for sure, so why waste your energy worrying about it?

Then one night when most of the ship was fast asleep, the alarm sounded. We had already held a number of drills, so the sound was not an unfamiliar one, though so far all our drills had been held in the daytime.

I raced with Garnet for the assembly hall, where the intercom was directing all non-essential personnel to gather. The hall was half-filled when we reached it. Scores of sleepy, half-dressed or still pajama-clad people were speculating about the cause for the midnight alarm. Speculation tended to put the blame on Marshall Lynch. But he had been a day and a half to our rear when we went to bed. Even if he opened up his throttles, he couldn't reach us that fast.

Boston appeared on the podium looking sleepy, not from having been rudely awakened as much as from not having slept at all. His eyes had dark rings under them. His gray hair, what there was of it, was disheveled, no doubt from his having run his hand through it all night. He called for attention.

"Fellow citizens," he began in a voice that sounded old and tired. "I won't play games with you. It's been no secret that Marshall Lynch—former President Lynch—has been dogging our tail ever since we left the solar quadrant of the galaxy. We've had no way of knowing what he wants from us. He might be looking for a free ride to our new home where he hopes to set himself up as chief honcho. Or he might choose to destroy us as soon as he learns where that new planet might be. "Whatever his intention, we've all lived in fear for several weeks now. Well, tonight, we learned something which, I'm afraid, will not do much to alleviate that fear.

"A small spacecraft, almost certainly from Lynch's fleet, was detected a short while ago on out scanners. It's moving at an unprecedented speed and will be approaching us within the hour. So far we've received no communication from it.

"I want to stress, though," he said, "that we have no reason to assume on the face of it that this craft intends us any harm. Presumably, it is coming on some kind of negotiating mission. What the issues—or demands—of that mission might be are unknown. Your guess is as good as mine."

"When did you spot it?" someone asked. Despite Mneh's religious conversion, the ship had continued to be run on a democratic model, in keeping with the tone of equality for all creatures agreed upon at the outset.

"Less than an hour ago," Boston said. "It somehow slipped through our scanners."

"Have we tried to make contact with it?" someone else asked.

"We have. There was no response."

A Simminoid was recognized and began signing with a great deal of feeling.

"For those of you who couldn't see," Boston said, "our brother asks what Moses Mneh is planning to do about the situation." He paused and glanced slowly around the auditorium. "Mneh believes…and I want you all to please accept this with an open mind for the moment." His face was flushed. It was the first time I had seen him show any hesitancy about Mneh's competence as our leader. "Mneh asks us to have trust…in God."

Chapter Nine

While the meeting was still in progress, a second alarm sounded. A wave of panic swept through the crowd. Someone began to demand his medication—the quick, effective tranquilizers that used to shield us from this dreadful feeling of fear. In theory, all medications, apart from those that cured physical illness, had been left on Earth. In reality, some had found their way onto the ship and could still be obtained "for a price." Someone hustled the panicky citizen out of the assembly hall before his terror set off a chain reaction.

Boston was conferring with one of the aides who had just appeared at his side. A few moments later he held up his hands for silence. "Fellow citizens!" he cried. "Please. Your attention!"

The lights dimmed and a half-size projection from the holovision materialized beside him. The images were those of Mneh and a couple of his assistants. Boston left the stage, and a few moments later his own image appeared beside that of Mneh, AKA Moses.

They were seated in a conference room, apparently waiting for something to happen, just as we were. Then the image vanished and a two-dimensional projection replaced it—a picture of a spacecraft. The markings clearly identified it as one of the NWC, not that we had had much doubt about that anyway. At first it was hard to tell how far away it was. But then we saw it fire its retros as it prepared to put alongside the Ark.

A second wave of fear, this time mixed with indignation,

passed through the crowd. We could afford to feel indignation now because it was apparent that the craft did not intend to simply blow us out of space.

Presumably a conversation was taking place between the Ark and this envoy from Marshall Lynch. But for whatever the reason we were not privy to it. All we could do was watch as the smaller ship edged closer and finally locked against our starboard hull. Then the picture vanished and the original holovision projection reappeared.

Two envoys, a man and a woman dressed in NWC uniforms, entered the conference room and greeted the ship's leaders. "We are here on official business from President Lynch," they announced.

Boston invited them to sit down. They both eyed Mneh and the other Simms warily before taking their seats. The envoy addressed all of his remarks to Boston and the other human present. "Our President," he said, stressing the possessive pronoun, "sends you greetings and sincere wishes that all aboard your ship are well and in good spirits."

Boston nodded. He glanced at Mneh who was following this interchange carefully but silently.

"You may return the same wishes from us to Marshall Lynch," Boston said. A murmur of disapproval bubbled through the assembly hall.

"We congratulate you also on your timely departure from our planet," the woman continued, including the two Simms this time in her smile. Only the slightest trace of revulsion betrayed what her real feelings must have been. But she was probably so full of mood-stabilizers, she could have held a cordial conversation with a corpse and not blinked an eyelash. "It's regrettable that those who were predicting just such a calamity did not receive a better hearing than they did."

"That was hardly our fault," Boston said.

The woman bowed her head in acknowledgment. "That's

true. The fault rests where it belongs—with the advisers who were supposed to keep the President abreast of such matters."

So that was to be their tack: It wasn't Lynch's fault the planet got blown out of the galaxy. It was his advisers'. Even if I were inclined to believe her implausible apology, my own experience contradicted it. I had told Lynch what was going to happen after personally witnessing the supernova's devastation on Alpha-II. His response was to lock me up in a mental institution.

I looked around at my neighbors. Most were scoffing at the images on the stage.

Boston asked the young woman—quite an attractive young woman at that—if she expected him to believe that the entire government was involved in a conspiracy to keep knowledge of the super nova from the President.

"No," she replied calmly. "Not the entire government. Just a few traitors. The very few that Marshall Lynch happened to trust implicitly."

"What, if I may ask then, was the information on which Mr. Lynch did act—or failed to act?"

"Of course you may ask," the woman's male counterpart said. "I think at this juncture we all have a right to ask that question, and to get a straight answer too."

I heard murmurs of approval from the people around me.

"The President was assured, not by one person but by several of his top science advisors, that there was nothing at all to the speculation about an exploding supernova. These people were not petty politicians, mind you, or even political appointees. They were some of the best minds in the Confederacy who were serving, supposedly, in the public interest. They all could have been earning more money in private industry."

Boston frowned. "I don't think I classify as 'one of the best minds in NWC,' but the signs were clear enough to me as well as to any number of my colleagues. But, for trying to warn our government of its impending demise we were summarily silenced.

How does Mr. Lynch explain that?"

The young man nodded gravely. "There's a great deal yet to be explained. And one of the reasons we've come to your ship is to tell you that the President would very much like to have the opportunity to do so personally."

"He wants to come aboard the Ark?"

"He wants to speak with you in person, with all of you, if possible."

"And if we decline that invitation?"

The two envoys remained perfect icons of tolerance.

"The President does not wish to impose himself upon anyone. If that is the consensus, he will respect it."

"Until when?"

"What do you mean?"

"He'll respect it for now, because he hardly has any other choice but to blow us into kingdom come, or he'll wait until we land somewhere and then take control? Either way he gets to sit in the driver's seat."

"Mr. Lynch would like to remain your President. However, if you no longer wish him to serve you in that capacity, he is quite willing to abide by your judgment—as long as it is arrived at democratically."

"Well, I think you'd better tell Marshal Lynch that we'll have to think over his generous offer and maybe hold a referendum on it."

"How long do you think that will take?"

"Do you have another engagement?"

"I beg your pardon?"

"Tell him we'll get right to work on it."

We waited anxiously for Boston to return to the assembly hall. In the interim, a debate took place on the floor—rather, several debates—clusters of hot opinion arguing the pros and cons of the situation. Finally someone had the good sense to suggest that we discuss the issue in a more orderly fashion. This was agreed to, and so began our first interstellar town meeting.

An elderly woman began by urging us not to be taken in by the emissaries' seeming benevolence. "I'm old enough to remember the old Union," she said, her long gray hair reaching almost to her waist. "I worked with Lynch and his people to overthrow that regime. Well, let me tell you something, citizens. Apart from a brief interlude, the old Union and the New Worlds Confederacy are as alike as two peas in a pod. All they did was change the name of the government agencies. The Secret Intelligence Agency became the New Worlds Information Service, but they didn't bother to change the departmental manuals. All they did was insert a new denominator into the auto-brain.

"Marshall Lynch was never a revolutionary. He was a good little general under the old regime. It isn't taught in the history courses some of you younger people took, but it was Lynch and his henchmen who put down the first uprisings against the Union before he decided to take control of the government himself.

"So don't look to him for fair dealing or any sense of responsibility for what happened on Earth. A man like him has one thing and one thing only on his mind. Power. All he can get of it." She looked around the auditorium. "I feel like a damned fool having to say these things after what we've all been through, after what each of us has already risked to get away from that man and his madness."

The next speaker supported what the first had said. "But there's one big fact my sister failed to acknowledge," he added. "And that is that we are at the mercy of Marshall Lynch and his fleet at the moment. We may speak all we like about his deviousness and personal ambition, but do we have any real choice except to deal with him?"

"Yes!" the first speaker responded. "We can tell him to go to hell and take our chances, just like we did back on Earth."

"It seems to me," the man replied, "that defiance is all well and good. But we're hardly in any position to be defiant. It seems to me we're more like a mouse being played with by a big cat. It may appear that he only wants to play, but he has no intention of letting us get away, and as a matter of fact he can tear us limb from limb any time he so chooses.

"Please don't get me wrong," he said. "I personally have no truck with Marshall Lynch or any of his people. But I do want to go on living." He looked carefully around the hall, which had grown very quiet. "Why, we haven't even been told what our destination is! How do we know we even have one? How do we know that we won't go on drifting through space forever? Does it make sense to wage a war of principle with Lynch when, essentially, we're in the same boat as he is?"

"Lynch is not to be trusted!" the woman cried.

"I agree," the speaker. "I don't propose that we even try to trust him. I only suggest that we not try to wage war against him."

The man was applauded as he stepped down from the stage. His face was a familiar one. He had been one of my first reading students back in the caverns on Earth. He was a fast learner and became one of the most regular users of the ship's library. His tastes ran to history and political science.

"What do the other ships think?" someone called out. "Shouldn't someone be sounding them out?"

"Excellent idea," Sheba said, suddenly appearing on the stage. I hadn't seen her for weeks. I had begun to wonder why she was keeping so much to herself. "As a matter of fact, a bulletin is being prepared right now for transmission. Of course, the other ships are not as literate as we are, so it will take some time to translate all of this into auto-brain. And auto-brains, as we all know, were not especially adept in the language of politics."

One of the great drawbacks of symbolic language, the only kind we learned how to "read," apart from hobbyists such as myself, was its inability to express anything another auto-brain could not comprehend. The brains were set up for mechanical

74

and administrative purposes. Political theory was well beyond their competence. Some of the cleverer people I had known sometimes made queer metaphors out of brainspeech to express a thought that the brain itself could not—would not—understand. But these mostly took the form of jokes or party stories.

I had a question of my own to ask.

"Sheba," I said, standing up, "why haven't we been told our destination?"

Her almost black eyes searched the crowd. When they found me, she smiled. "Walter," she said, "where have you been keeping yourself? Please don't run away after the meeting," she said, as if I weren't standing in the midst of a huge crowd of people. "But to answer your question, I don't know. I myself certainly haven't been told our destination. Presumably, Mneh and his navigator know. I suppose the idea is to minimize the number of people with this knowledge so that in a contingency precisely like the one we are here to discuss, with Marshall Lynch breathing down our necks, that information would not be readily available to him either."

"But we do have a destination?" I persisted.

"I think that's safe to assume."

I waited for her after the meeting broke up. We took a stroll down one of the lesser-used passageways.

"Look here, Walter," she said, "what do you make of this religious business Mneh is involved in?"

I had assumed she wanted to confer about Marshall Lynch's attempt at diplomacy, but I only hesitated for a second before giving her my answer. "I think it's a crock of nonsense."

"I'm glad I'm not the only one on this ship who thinks that."

"You agree?"

"Of course I do. I may not be a sage myself, Walter, but I'm not about to believe that some supernatural being is going to get us out of the mess we're in. If we do survive, it will be thanks to our own doing."

Her dark brown skin was bright with strong feeling.

"I just assumed that you…."

"…bought it hook, line, and sinker, like Boston is trying to do? Give me credit for some brains. Boston has his own reasons for putting up with the old bird's hallucinations. Walter, you and I have never really talked as friends before, but maybe now is the time to start. We have too much at stake not to," she said, indicating the cafeteria, where we could talk with more anonymity than in the ship's passageways.

We sat down with cups of tea.

"Boston is a man driven very much by his own particular needs," she said. "We all are, of course. But this business about Mneh and his visions fits in very nicely with a tendency I've noticed in my husband before. Boston's a very bright man. You could say that he's a genius. But he's not a leader, Walt. Not a number-one man. He can take orders, originate new ideas and execute them well—but always under the aegis of someone else, someone he believes in implicitly. And that person has been Mneh. Boston worked like a dog for that Simm on Earth. Without him, the Movement never would have gotten anywhere among the human population. And without the humans and their accessibility to technology, how far do you think the Simms would have gotten on their own?

"Down deep, he probably doesn't subscribe to Mneh's 'conversion' any more than you or I. But he wants to believe. Desperately. And he'll go on wanting to believe as long as he can. Because he needs Mneh. He needs that old ape," she said, the corners of her mouth suddenly falling, "more than he needs me."

For a moment I thought she was going to cry. We rarely got to see tears on Earth. Our daily dose precluded any such display of emotion. I watched with fascination as two tiny droplets formed in the corner of each of her dark eyes. The drops grew larger, then broke free and ran rapidly down her cheeks.

Chapter Ten

No one laid eyes on Boston or on any of the other people close to Mneh for the next twenty-four hours. We were told they were planning strategy. Meanwhile, I was relieved of my duties as librarian and given a job on the bridge monitoring radiation and standing ready in case Lynch decided to force the issue.

The rest of the fleet was canvassed and, by the end of the second day, had held their own meetings and reported back to the Ark. All except one vessel voted not to allow Lynch to address us. The sole dissenter was a ship from the Orion space colony. Lynch had liberated them from the United Planets during the civil war. Orion was a prize for anyone to get hold of. They had been responsible for much of the asteroid mining operations going on in the system. Lynch was no fool. Without Orion the supply of raw materials for his war machine would have been in serious jeopardy. Orion rewarded him with its eternal gratitude.

A communiqué was drawn up and transmitted to Lynch's ship. For several hours there was no response. I was standing the night watch, passing the time with a book of crossword puzzles that I had discovered at the bottom of a crate from the ship's library. The comm board had been silent all afternoon and evening. The other ships were no doubt as anxious as we were for Lynch's response. But, for the sake of keeping all channels open, they were maintaining a communications blackout.

At 9:30 I was relieved for my break. The ship was quieting down for the night. The cafeteria was almost deserted. But expectation hung heavy in the air, and ship's silence seemed eerie this particular evening. I finished my snack and hurried back to the bridge long before my time had elapsed.

My co-watch didn't seem surprised to see me back so soon.

"Weird down there, ain't it?" he said, turning from the big comm board, which was still dark except for the occasional fields of radiation we passed through.

I sat down beside him and began to do a particle count.

"How long do you think this will last?"

"Beats me," I said. "I guess it could go on for the rest of the trip if Lynch sticks to his promise. But I wouldn't count on it."

We went on to other topics—the ship's ping-pong tournament, a history book we shared a common interest in.

Suddenly the board lit up.

The comm man opened up the channel and few seconds later Marshall Lynch's face appeared on the screen.

"Ladies and gentlemen," someone announced just as if we were still back on Earth. "The President of the New Worlds Confederacy."

Lynch waited for a cue, then smiled brightly and said, "My fellow Confederates."

By prearrangement the signal was piped throughout the ship. Just in case any of the other ships was having trouble picking up the transmission, we were relaying it to them as well.

"These are, to say the least, unusual circumstances under which I address you this evening.

"We have all endured much, and yet we all have a great deal to look forward to, thanks to the clear-headedness and brave resolution of some of our citizens. Let me be the first to admit—and, believe me, I do so with a profound sense of humility for what was allowed to transpire on our home planets—let me be the first to admit that I must bear primary responsibility for the shameless lies which kept us from knowing about the impending disaster in time to evacuate more than a handful of our citizens.

"You, my fellow citizens, were more prudent than I. Some of you saw through the fabrications with which my most trusted advisors deceived me day after day. As a military man who came to public office much against my will, I did not have the scientific training necessary to refute such bogus advice. A president, like any public official, must rely upon his trusted advisors to guide him and the nation through the turbulent waters of scientific argument.

"To my everlasting shame and dishonor, I, your President, relied upon the wrong ones.

"I was deceived by men and women who, on the surface, appeared to be working in the national interest but whose real allegiance was not to the people of the New Worlds Confederacy but to a network of interplanetary corporations which preferred to see the entire solar system atomized rather than abandon their investment, even if that meant the loss of their own lives."

This was vintage Lynch. But something told me those corporate executives he was alluding to were sitting right behind him while he begged us for absolution.

It was amazing how much like his old self he looked. His forte had always been taking responsibility for little setbacks so that when a victory materialized that he knew was just around the corner he could be right there to claim all the credit. As he went on to detail the perfidy of his advisors, I thought back twenty years to when I was a boy of ten and the civil war was in its final bloody months. Could this be the same man I had idolized, as did so many others of my generation? Was this the man who liberated Mars and Titan and even brought the war to the nearest stars, until every contingent of the rebel Union was either destroyed or had surrendered?

It was only after I visited Alpha Centauri myself and saw the results of the kind of warfare Lynch had waged that my image of him began to tarnish. Neutron war had been outlawed for more than a hundred years. There was certainly no call for its use in the Centaurian system where, at best, a handful of rebels had been holding out. And yet Lynch had saturated all the Centaurian planets with deadly radiation, destroying every form of mammalian life, including thousands of children and their guardians holed up in deep underground bunkers that failed to shield them adequately from the powerful rays. Sissy was one of the lucky few who survived.

"In conclusion, my fellow Confederates, I ask only that you give me the chance to make amends to you and, through you, to our brethren who perished on Earth and on the colonies of the NWC.

"We need each other, every man, woman and child—and, yes, even our Simms, for I am aware that they were instrumental in helping you to achieve the remarkable evacuation you accomplished.

"I do not speak tonight as one threatening you with the might of my interstellar fleet. I do not come to you with recriminations or ultimatums. I come rather as your President, the President of all of our citizens. When the day comes—and I wish it to come soon just as you do—that we can all gather under one roof on our new home planet and hold elections for a new national assembly, I will abide by whatever choice you decide to make. You have my word on that.

"But until that cherished day arrives, I only ask that as good citizens of the NWC you accept your responsibility to the nation and to each other, just as I accept mine to you."

One more big smile, and the image vanished.

"What do you think?" the comm man asked.

"I think we're in for a lot of trouble," I said. "That was one of the coolest threats I've ever seen. Lynch certainly hasn't lost his touch. 'I love you all, my children. Please don't make me blast you into oblivion.'"

"You think it will come to that?"

"It will if we don't knuckle under and let him have his way. You don't think he made that reference to his warships just to expend his breath, do you? This is the showdown."

The next move was ours. Lynch was obviously not going to take no for an answer and we were not about to say yes. The only alternative, the leadership council decided after a full night of deliberation, was to string him along as best we could and hope for a brighter idea that wouldn't jeopardize our independence.

The council was still working on the wording of its reply when Lynch decided to take matters into his own hands. A blip showed up on our scanner. A half hour later Lynch's private space sled was asking for docking instructions.

"What do we do now?" I asked the man who had come to the bridge to relieve me. Technically, I was off duty. But I was not about to sit in my room and do more crosswords while the fate of the last vestiges of the human, and other, races hung in the balance.

"It's up to Mneh, I guess," the man replied.

A few moments later, Mneh, Boston and Sheba and two other members of the council came onto the bridge.

"Where is he?" Boston said.

"Just off to starboard. You can almost see him through the window."

Boston glanced quickly at the comm board.

"Hold him off for a minute. Ask them to repeat their transmission on another channel."

"What difference will that make?" Sheba asked. "If we turn him away he'll come back with a gunboat. Lynch is determined to have his way. The best we can hope for is a compromise. That's what we should be working out now instead of standing here like a bunch of trapped rats."

Boston glared back at her. It was the first time I had seen any disharmony between them. Mneh noticed the pot beginning to boil and intervened.

"Maybe Sheba's right," he signed to the flight commander. "We can't resist his armor. We may as well try to reason with him. He probably won't try to dictate to us until we've led him to a habitable planet. Let's work out a deal we can live with—temporarily. What do you say, Boston? Give me your honest opinion."

This sounded more like the old Mneh.

Boston regarded him for several moments before replying. "You're right. There's nothing else we can do."

Chapter Eleven

I asked for and was given permission to accompany the council members to the conference room where Lynch was being received. This would be the first time I had laid eyes on the man since I had been brought to his office following my return from Alpha-II with news about the supernova. Officially, I was there now as ship's historian. But I had my own reasons for being present.

He came marching in attended by two beefy generals sporting so many medals, clusters and whatnot it was a wonder they could support the weight. They made a very shady-looking trio.

"Please be seated," he invited us, flashing the benign smile we had seen earlier on the video.

"I'd like to introduce our council," Boston said and proceeded to make the rounds, starting with Sheba and working his way around the table until at last he came to Mneh and the Simm seated at Mneh's side.

"And this, Mr. President, is Moses Mneh, our council leader."

Lynch's eyebrows went up a notch. No doubt he had heard reports about renegade Simms. But this may have been the first time he saw one in the flesh, hirsute and naked. The idea that an ape was heading our expedition would no doubt be the hardest pill for him to swallow.

Mneh bowed his head and signed, "My pleasure, Mr. President."

The irony was lost on Lynch.

"Indeed," he replied.

The other Simm was introduced, and we all sat down.

"Let's not beat about the bush," Lynch began, spreading his hands open on the table. His two generals, one on either side, sat ramrod straight, only their eyes moving. "We need each other far too much not to cooperate.

"I realize we've had our differences. But surely, under the circumstances, we can learn to live together and make a new start."

He might have been suggesting a marital reconciliation. I doubted that he remembered who I was when Boston introduced me. He must have thrown scores of people such as myself into dungeons of one kind or another over the past several months. As he spoke now, I studied his manner and expression. His smile was warm, his appeal seemed genuine. I realized the attraction he must have held for voters when he was running for office. That charm must also have come in handy when he was trying to cajole—instead of sledgehammer—someone into seeing things his way, as he was doing with us now.

"Mr. President," Boston said. "I speak for our council leader, Moses Mneh, as well as for the majority of the ship's passengers." Mneh nodded approvingly. Lynch regarded him warily. "It's no secret that we owe our present position to the shortsightedness of your administration, which you already spoke of in your address to the fleet a short while ago. However, nothing can alter the past and we have to make the most of the present and, hopefully, the future as well.

"But we know you didn't come here to establish diplomatic relations."

Lynch laughed. Then he turned to the generals beside him. They dutifully laughed along with their commander.

"I hardly think so," he said, including all of us this time in his forced smile. "But I appreciate your frankness, Mr. Boston.

You're perfectly right. I did not come here to establish diplomatic relations. I came here to re-establish relations between our citizenry and its legally elected government. I was elected your President, and I intend to go on serving as your President until the end of my term."

He managed to say all that without the slightest diminution of that engaging smile. The man could have slit all our throats and still gone on smiling.

Mneh stirred. "Are we to consider that an ultimatum?"

For a moment Lynch looked as if the table or a chair had spoken. He glanced toward Boston, then toward myself, then considered the Simm again with ill-disguised distaste. "Gentlemen—and lady—" he said, nodding at Sheba, "I'm as open-minded as the next man. But surely you don't expect me to negotiate with a Simminoid. No disrespect to yourself, Mr....ah, Minn, was it?"

"Mneh," I said, drawing Lynch's eyes my way. They narrowed as they took in my face again.

"Haven't we met somewhere?"

"We certainly have," I said. "I was one of those who warned you about the supernova. You put me into a mental hospital for my trouble."

Lynch frowned as if trying to recall any such incident. "That was no doubt the doing of one of those advisors I mentioned in my speech. I sincerely apologize."

"As far as negotiating with a Simminoid is concerned," I went on, "I can tell you that Moses Mneh was responsible for saving all our necks—which is more than can be said for your government, Mr. President."

"But surely," Lynch protested, addressing himself to Boston, "a Simminoid is not a citizen. Why, he's not even human!"

"Have humans performed in a manner that gives them a corner on the meaning of the word 'humanity'?" Sheba said. Lynch and she were about the same shade of brown, only Lynch's eyes were bright blue. "We've just finished destroying the entire solar system, or allowing it to be destroyed by our inaction. We damned near destroyed it twenty years ago during the war. Is that what you mean by 'humanity'?"

"But, Miss…. As much as I can agree with you—up to a point—that hardly means we should turn everything over to the animals."

"They couldn't botch it up any worse than we have."

Lynch opened his hands in an appeal for sanity to the other human members on the council. But we just stared back at him.

"Mneh is our leader," Boston said. "If you can't accept that, I don't think we can have any kind of meaningful dialogue."

This was a lot for Lynch to swallow. He struggled with it for a moment, turning various shades of red beneath his darker complexion. Then he suddenly stopped struggling. "All right, this has gone far enough," he said, without the warm smile and avuncular manner. "I've got six gunboats and three fleetships out there. I can blow you out of the sky in less time than it takes to draw two breaths. You either play ball with me, get these Simms back in cages where they belong, or face the music."

He stood up abruptly. His two generals, as if attached to him with string, stood up a split second behind him. "I'll give you two hours to think it over."

Lynch returned to his fleet to await our decision. We continued to sit in the conference room, looking at each other. We were all very scared, but no one wanted to show it.

Finally Mneh broke the deadlock. "The Lord will provide."

We looked at him, not with rancor, not with disbelief, not even with the humoring condescension we had shown his religious pronouncements before. We actually regarded him with gratitude. At least he had something to hang on to, while the rest of us were awash in panic. We regarded him as a starving man does a heaping plate of food—with no inclination to determine if this is the real thing or only another mirage produced by his own hunger.

Another assembly was hastily called. The meeting with Lynch was reported and the floor thrown open for discussion.

None of us doubted that what Lynch wanted was total and unquestioned acknowledgment of his authority. He would probably be content for now to let us pretend to go on leading the way, but he wanted some sign of subservience. That sign, apparently, was to be a disavowal of the Simms. Lynch was from the old school. His specism was ingrained. No doubt it was the shock of finding a Simm at the helm of the Ark that caused him to blow his cool in the conference room. We had substituted an ape for him.

There was a general consensus to oppose Lynch's demands. What was surprising was that there was any dissent at all. But a small vocal minority expressed quite passionately what many more of us had in the back of our minds: Maybe we should, temporarily, bow to Lynch on the matter of the Simms if it meant saving theirs as well as our own skins. What was the point to idealism if it only got us killed?

After the meeting Sheba and I discussed the matter further.

"How far are we from a habitable star?" I asked.

"I don't know. Really," she assured me when she saw the hint of skepticism in my face, "I don't. Neither does Boston. I don't think even Mneh knows."

"Then, how the devil are we ever going to get there?"

"I didn't say no one knows. You see, we anticipated a contingency like this one—I mean Lynch or some other despot tailing us. So we decided not to entrust our destination to any of the leaders, at least not deliberately."

"This is making no sense."

"What would happen if, say, you or I knew our destination and Lynch decided to interrogate us?"

"He'd get it out of me, most likely."

"Correct. And that contingency was exactly what we anticipated, wisely, as it turned out. So we held a lottery. This was before you joined the Movement. The star we would head for was indicated by its constellation symbol on a card and dropped into a hopper containing hundreds of other cards. We all drew a card blindly from the hopper. Everyone except two people drew a blank—or gibberish. Two of us got the actual constellation."

"How do you know those two people are trustworthy?"

"We don't. One of them—even both—may betray us. But at least those two people are anonymous, unlike Mneh, Boston and myself. Lynch probably thinks you know our destination as well. What he doesn't know is that, no matter what he does to any of us, he won't find it out. Unless, of course, one of us four actually drew that card."

"But what about the person, or persons, who decided on that particular star in the first place? They know as well, don't they?"

"We had an auto-brain do it. Then we destroyed its memory."

Well, at least now I knew why we seemed to be flying blind across the universe. But suppose the people with the knowledge of our destination were among those who were willing to return the Simms to their previous condition of servitude, as Lynch was demanding? Wouldn't they also be willing to volunteer our destination in order to save their skins?

I returned to my post on the bridge, wondering how I had gotten into this mess in the first place. But when I recalled what the alternative would have been, even the prospect of a protracted confrontation with Lynch and his gunboats seemed preferable.

The two hours were almost up. Mneh, Boston, Sheba and the other members of the council came onto the bridge to witness the transmission of our reply to Lynch's fleetship. There was none of the usual ship's chatter. The communications officer went about setting up the channel with silent efficiency. Contact was established. The comm man looked over his shoulder and waited for instruction.

"Tell them Marshall Lynch's demand is unacceptable," Boston said. "The Simminoids will remain as they are."

The operated banged out the message on the board, then waited for further instruction.

"Tell him also that, if they still want to cooperate with us, we are willing to enter into negotiations. Nothing, however, is to be presupposed. We negotiate as equals. Majority rules."

The second part of the message was sent. Then we waited for the reply. It wasn't long in coming.

"President Lynch requests a second conference. Please send two negotiators—no Simms. A sled will be by to pick them up within an hour."

A sigh of qualified relief. We had been braced for sudden extinction. Mneh had begun to pray. Instead, the old fox Lynch wanted to parlay.

To be on the safe side, we decided that the two negotiators should swear before leaving that neither of them possessed knowledge of our destination, just in case Lynch decided to get rough. Knowing where a habitable star was likely to be was still our best card in dealing with Lynch. As long as we had that information and he didn't, he would not destroy us.

Sheba and I immediately volunteered. There was no way of knowing for sure if Boston or Mneh had drawn one of the two destination cards. Besides, the more quickly two people volunteered, the more anonymous the actual card holders would remain. Lynch might try, and succeed, in extracting information from two of us, but he was not likely to take on the entire fleet.

The sled arrived. We embraced the others and joined Lynch's pilots waiting for us in the pressure lock. They saluted us as if we were visiting heads of state, but I didn't put much stock in their deference. Lynch could cut or cajole, depending on what the circumstances called for.

The flight to the war fleet was quick and uneventful. The

sky looked utterly unfamiliar. A huge red giant glowed like a terrestrial sunset less than a light year away. On Earth it might still appear as a healthy white light in the night sky—if there were a night sky or an Earth from which to view it. Otherwise, there was only void, that terrible empty silence that no spacedog, no matter how experienced, ever gets used to. Even when it no longer strikes a primitive terror into your heart, it goes on clutching at your intestines and makes your brain reel with its yawning absurdity. You soon learn that to look directly into it is as foolish as to turn your eyes toward the sun.

Finally the white dots of Lynch's fleet appeared in the vacuum, pinpoints of light like the moons of Jupiter viewed through a child's telescope. The pilot fired his retro and we slowed imperceptibly.

A welcoming party greeted us on the other side of the space lock, led by Lynch's second-in-command, Hassim Dupré. I recognized him from his pictures. He showed us into a more sumptuous version of the conference room aboard our own ship.

"The President extends his greetings and regrets that he is not able to meet with you personally at this point," he told us in his precise but slightly accented idiom. "He looks forward, however, to meeting with all of us following the conclusion of a mutually satisfactory understanding."

Pure grease. In a few words he had laid out our fate for us. Dupré had served as chief of Lynch's administrative staff. Apparently, he was not one of those "advisors" who had fed the President inaccurate information about the supernova.

We sat down at a shiny black conference table and were immediately fed canapés and served carafes of tempting beverages by Simms dressed in the traditional servant's outfits. Their shaved bodies were held stiffly erect by rigorous back braces. There was no trace of interest in their eyes. We might have been any anonymous group of humans in the service of Lynch and his cohorts.

"Please help yourselves," Dupré encouraged, apparently taking such a sumptuous display of food for granted. "I've just eaten, otherwise I would join you."

I nibbled at something that looked like bean curd but had a sharper taste. Sheba tried the pickled vegetables. We both avoided the beverages. Dupré watched us with amusement. He looked much older than his holograms. His skin had the texture of animal hide and was wrinkled like the skin of old people who spend a lot of time in the sun. His eyes, though, were bright with intelligence. His mother had been a world-famous dancer. His father was a prize-winning chemist.

"Can we begin, Mr. Dupré?" Sheba asked finally. "I think we'd all like to get this over with."

Dupré bowed graciously and nodded to a Simm to take the food away. "I like your frankness, Miss Sheba."

"Sheba will do."

"Sheba, then. I appreciate that quality in both men and women. Too frequently I deal with diplomatic imprecision, and slip into it myself on occasion."

Sheba allowed him a polite smile. He seemed satisfied.

"I trust you understand why President Lynch invited you to his fleetship."

"More or less," I said. "I believe we made clear our position about the Simms."

Dupré directed his smile my way.

"Indeed," he said. "I'm afraid you've made your position perhaps even clearer than you meant to."

"Have we?"

"I was thinking of the President's reaction. You might, you know, have softened the blow a bit."

"How could we have done that—apart from doing what he asked, putting the Simms 'back in their cages,' as he put it?"

My eyes wandered toward the two Simminoids standing at a discreet distance from the table, their bodies held unnaturally erect like waiters in an expensive restaurant. Our conversation was having no apparent effect on them.

"The President," Dupré went on, "can become testy at times, as I'm sure you've noticed."

"Meaning?" Sheba asked.

"Meaning only that he surely would not have invited you here if he wished to gain your allegiance merely by force or even by ultimatum. If he had wanted that, there is certainly enough fire power in this fleet to destroy us all many times over.

"In any case, I think it was extremely wise of you to accept. And I want you both to know that I personally breathed a great sigh of relief when you did so."

That was how it went for the first hour. The man was a genius of dissembling, refusing either to be challenged or angered. He agreed to any point of view we expressed, then "regretted" or "feared" that the consequences of such an idea might not be acceptable to the President. It was my first experience dealing with an experienced diplomat, and I found it infuriating. After sixty minutes of this cat-and-mouse game, he suggested that we take a break and offered to show us around the fleetship.

He led us out of the conference room and down a long corridor lined by offices and control stations. Then the corridor suddenly opened out onto a balcony. Below it stretched a huge greenhouse attached to the main ship by gangways at a lower level. The greenhouse itself was essentially a freely suspended system, shielded on three sides. The overhead was exposed to the sky, or rather to a series of condensers which gathered the available starlight and passed it on to the growing things below. It made our own system look like a backyard garden.

"As you see, we have everything we need, for the moment."

As I looked down from the overhanging balcony, I saw a flock of chickens pecking at the edge of a bean patch. The entire ecosystem must have encompassed several acres.

"It provides us with something better than space rations which, as I'm sure you know, pale after a month or two."

We couldn't help a nod of agreement.

We walked down to the lower level. There the scene more closely resembled our own ship's. The chief difference was in the quality of the materials from which it was constructed. Ours was a slapdash, spare-parts affair. Lynch's was constructed of the latest materials and designed specifically for extended space flight. It was downright plush.

There were Simms all over. Just as they had done on Earth, they continued to tend the vegetable gardens and care for the animals. They kept the ship clean, monitored some of its simpler systems and waited on the human crew and passengers. They did so without any sign of rancor or resentment. I wondered if any of them had ever heard of Mneh's Movement. But each time we drew close to one of them, Dupré either put himself between us and the Simm or ordered the Simm to do something that took him or her out of our immediate area.

Our tour ended at the gymnasium where a score of healthy human bodies were swimming, lifting weights and playing various games with balls of different shapes and sizes. Most of them were young. The women were all exceptionally attractive. When I commented on this to Dupré, he laughed and quoted an Arabic proverb about an ugly woman being twice as much nuisance as a sick camel.

"That was very interesting," Sheba said after we had sat down again, this time in a kind of study furnished with soft furniture and even a fake fireplace. "But what does it have to do with the purpose of our visit?"

Dupré settled into the thick arms of a leather club chair and joined his hands together on his chest.

"A fair question," he said. "A very fair question. And, as a matter of fact, it has everything indeed to do with the purpose of your visit."

He regarded each of us carefully for a moment, then asked, "Have your scanners picked up anything unusual lately?"

Sheba and I exchanged questioning looks. "Unusual how?"

Dupré took a deep breath and contemplated the ceiling over his head.

"I'm thinking of a rather large mass of material to the starboard."

No response from our side. Our scanners were, no doubt, not as powerful as the scanners of a first-line fleetship. Dupré knew that.

"It looks like high-grade metal. Possibly a deposit of helium as well. It might even contain some uranium." He removed his eyes from the ceiling and confronted us again. "You realize of course what that means."

We did. Despite a pretty thorough recycling system, our resources would not last forever

"You'd like to farm it," I suggested.

He made a steeple out of his long fingers and pursed his lips into a reluctant kiss.

"But why put it that way, Mr. Centaurus? After all, aren't we all pretty much in the same fix? Surely your own supplies are not inexhaustible."

"If not, we have the capability to find more."

"True, true. But, under the circumstances, doesn't that seem just the slightest bit absurd? How many light-years are we from Earth? We are the only human beings left in perhaps the entire galaxy. Is there any good reason for us not to cooperate with each other?"

"You wouldn't be thinking," Sheba said, "of our superior numbers, Mr. Dupré? Not to mention the muscle-power of our Simminoids."

With his open hands Dupré made a gesture as old as the ages.

"Of course I would, Miss Sheba. And is that such a criminal thought? Does it make sense for us to go on disagreeing over insubstantial issues instead of pooling our mutual resources?"

"And what," I asked, "would such a cooperative venture cost us in terms of our freedom?"

Dupré regarded me with astonishment. "Your freedom? Surely you don't think I'm proposing anything that would endanger your rights as citizens of the NWC?"

"Never mind the Confederacy. That was blown to pieces weeks ago, thanks to Lynch."

"All right," he said. "Have it your way. But we both need those resources. A cooperative venture would simply be the most efficient way to get them. But if you prefer not to join us in the undertaking, or if you know something that would make such a detour unnecessary...." he added, searching our faces carefully through his artificial smile. "Let me be frank, Miss Sheba, Mr. Centaurus. Are we in fact close enough to our destination to preclude the necessity of having to renew our fuel supply and other resources? An honest reply would save us both a great deal of time and effort."

For a moment we sat staring back at him. Then I replied for both of us. "We have no idea what our destination is."

Dupré continued to regard us carefully for another moment, then closed his eyes and slowly nodded his head. "I see."

Chapter Twelve

We were invited to stay the night. Under the circumstances—we couldn't very well walk home—we agreed.

We were shown into a suite of three rooms, two bedrooms with a sitting room in between.

"Just like honeymooners," I said, after we had changed into the pajamas that were laid out on our beds. The remark was meant to help dispel some of the tension we both felt about being detained longer than we had hoped to be.

If I actually had been a bridegroom, I couldn't have wished for a more lovely bride. The bright red pajamas Sheba put on set off her dark complexion marvelously. She was a beautiful woman, very much in the prime of her maturity. She laughed at my observation, though, making us both feel a little easier.

"What did you make of our host?" I asked.

Her brow clouded. A few wrinkles appeared at the edges of her eyes. "I think they haven't made up their mind yet what to do. I'm sure Dupré didn't believe it when you told him we don't know the destination of the Ark. They'd like to get that information out of us, but they don't want to risk alienating the rest of our fleet.

"On the other hand, as long as they can continue to tail us, we will presumably lead them right to where they want to go. I would guess that at the moment all that's really at stake is Marshall Lynch's pride. The idea of being a follower infuriates him. The idea of following a Simminoid adds insult to injury."

I had to agree with her assessment of the situation. I didn't feel as confident, though, about Lynch's not using coercion because he feared alienating his loyal citizens any further than he already had. The very fact that we were about to bunk down on a warship instead of on the Ark amounted to coercion, as far as I was concerned.

Sure enough, just after 2:00 A.M. I was awakened by a discreet knock on my door. At first I thought it must be Sheba in the next room, unable to sleep. But then I realized that the rapping was coming from the door that opened onto the corridor outside.

"It's Hassim Dupré, Mr. Centaurus. I'm terribly sorry to disturb you, but something's come up that we'd like to talk with you about."

As much as I didn't like being disturbed in the middle of the night, it was the "we" that boded ill. I told him I would be right out, then splashed some cold water on my face and put on a robe I found hanging in the closet.

"What is it?" I asked sleepily.

"Just some medical business. Nothing to be alarmed about." He was still wearing the same suit he had had on when we met with him the previous afternoon. "Please follow me."

We passed through a series of corridors which led eventually to a part of the ship not included in our tour the previous day. Finally we reached a kind of hospital ward which I took to be the ship's infirmary. Some doctors or technicians in white lab coats were at work. They turned toward us as we entered, and one of them, a middle-aged woman with a brisk, authoritarian manner approached me.

"This is Dr. Nieves," Dupré said. "The ship's surgeon."

Even as Dupré spoke, the woman took hold of my wrist and began to monitor my pulse.

"What's this all about?"

"Nothing to be concerned about," she said, distending my

eyelids for a look inside. "Just a touch of space sickness going around. We want to make sure you don't bring any of it back to your fleet. Please take off your robe and roll up your sleeve."

It seemed to me that they might have waited till the morning. But "space sickness"—actually any number of different disorders that can effect someone after an extended journey through space—could be a serious matter if it got out of hand. It was a good idea to take preventive measures at the first sign.

She injected me with a vial containing some kind of orange fluid, then asked me to lie down in case I should develop an allergic reaction. I had never had a reaction in the past, but she said she wanted to make sure. "We wouldn't want your colleagues on the Ark to accuse us of medical malpractice, would we."

I lay down on a cot that must have doubled as a lounge for night-duty medical staff to take catnaps. I still hadn't completely come awake yet, and the temptation to doze off while I waited for the injection to take effect was very strong. I closed my eyes and listened to the shuffle and clinking noises of the medical staff as they went about their business in the infirmary. Soon the noises began to suggest images to my sleepy brain—a giant space ship in the shape of a whale, small white birds flying rapidly back and forth across an earthly meadow. Then I seemed to be in the meadow myself. The birds were actually trying to warn me about something. I looked up into the clear blue sky, and there was the giant whaleship, so immense that as it passed overhead it eclipsed the bright light of the sun. I ran for the shelter of the trees at the meadow's edge, but there was no escaping the giant ship. It descended until it hovered just above the treetops. I ran further into the woods, which had become a dense forest. The whale followed, pressing down closer and closer until it was touching the top branches of the trees. Then I realized that it was not a spaceship at all. It was a dirigible. If it punctured itself on a branch, it would collapse and fall on top of me.

I began searching for a place to hide. The small animals

that lived in the forest were also scurrying about, trying to get away from the ominous shadow above. A rabbit dived into his burrow at the base of a thick oak tree. I dived in too and, miraculously as befits a dream, managed to squeeze through the tiny hole.

On the other side was a brightly-lit room. Men and women in lab coats were preparing vials of orange liquid. I was back in the infirmary. Dr. Nieves was standing above me, taking my pulse.

"I think you'd better stay put for a while," she said, smiling ambiguously. "The serum I gave you has some properties you may not have experienced before. Best to lie quietly for a while."

I closed my eyes and soon had dozed off again. What happened next I'm still not sure of, but the "dreams" I had were unlike any others I've experienced.

It seemed that I was a child again. I did not especially feel like a child or see myself as it child. But everything around me conspired to make me believe that I was. The infirmary had become a nursery, almost identical to the one that I and the other children in my neighborhood had attended while our parents were at work. My clothing was that of a child. The doctor and the attendants were dressed in teachers' smocks. They smiled and invited me to play with a pile of colored blocks. The blocks reminded me of the blocks Boston had put end to end, day after day, in the mental hospital.

It was very pleasant being a child again, feeling things I hadn't felt since my toddler days—the friendly warmth of an adult's smile, the sense that play was all I need concern myself with. But I also knew that I was not a child, that the smiling adults around me had made some kind of dreadful mistake. At the same time I felt a great reluctance to disappoint them. They seemed so kind and loving, and I wanted their kindness and their love very badly.

I dangled my legs over the high bed and let myself slip down to the floor. My legs were wobbly, just as I imagined the legs of a toddler should be. I dropped to my knees and crawled across the floor to the pile of blocks the "teachers" were holding out to me. But instead of staying with me to join in my play, they retreated into a kind of box from which they observed me from what seemed a very high perspective. If I really was still an adult myself, I thought, how could they be so much bigger than I was?

I sat down next to the pile of blocks and began playing with them. I knew that something was expected of me, and I wanted very much not to disappoint the adults watching, so I began arranging the blocks into various shapes—a spaceship, a boat, a tall building. The "teachers" reacted with more smiles, but somehow I sense that this wasn't what they really wanted. So I dismantled what I had built and started over.

This time I made atomic structures. The adults showed more interest this time, so I went on building more and more elaborate atoms, pleased with the approval they were giving me but also afraid that they would finally realize I was really an adult and didn't deserve their praise.

Then it occurred to me that what would please them most would be a recreation of the constellation Boston had made in order to communicate with me in the mental hospital. I constructed the constellation Centaurus, feeling very proud at what a clever little tike I was.

They craned their necks eagerly to see what I was doing but remained inside their box where while I completed my project down to the last star and then looked up for their approval.

But instead of smiles they were frowning down at me. I was crestfallen. I had given my best effort, and failed.

The next thing I knew I was back in my room. It was late morning judging from the clock on my bedstand. My first thoughts were for Sheba. Had she also been taken away in the middle of the night? I jumped up from the bed, only to collapse on it again with a throbbing pain that threatened to split my head apart.

I sat up again, this time more slowly, then dangled my legs over the edge of the bed and gradually put some weight on my feet. My head still felt like it had a combustion engine inside. I had only a vague memory of being awakened in the middle of the night and brought to the infirmary.

I struggled into my robe and stumbled toward the door connecting with Sheba's bedroom. I knocked, gently at first, then more forcefully when she failed to respond. Finally I pressed the latch. The door slid back soundlessly. Sheba lay on her bed asleep, the bedcovers disarranged as if she had spent the night tossing and turning. I approached the bed and laid my hand gently on her shoulder.

"It's Walter. Are you all right?"

I shook her gently, then more vigorously until her eyes opened. She moaned.

"My head!"

"I know," I said, starting to remember what had happened to me. "I had a dose too."

She rolled over to face me, then clutched at the sides of her short-cropped hair. "What hit me?"

"The same thing that hit me. Some kind of truth serum. To get information out of us."

She moaned again. I went to get something cool to put on her forehead.

"This will help," I said, pressing a wet cloth to her temples.

After the throbbing in her head subsided, she asked, "Do you think they'll let us go back to the Ark?"

"They will if they have any faith in their own medicine. We had nothing to tell them."

I left her to dress, returning to my own room to sort things out. I had scarcely sat down when there was a knock on the door. It was a Simm bringing our breakfasts. He was virtually indistinguishable from the scores of other Simms we had seen aboard the ship. His waiter's uniform was identical to those that

Simms wore on Earth, right down to the high, stiff collar that forced them to keep their heads erect.

"Wait," I said as he turned to leave. "Don't you know that your brother Simms have revolted? Wouldn't you like to be free too? Wouldn't you like to stop wearing this ridiculous costume and simply go about in your own natural body? Do you want to go on being a slave for the rest of your life, until you get too old to be of any use and be put to sleep?"

Already well into middle age, the Simm stared back at me blindly. "Does Master require anything else?" he signed just as if I had said nothing. I studied his vacant expression. There was no sign of understanding in his eyes, no spark of even a desire to understand. Chemically, surgically or perhaps simply through years of habitual fear and conditioning, he had been rendered virtually brainless—exactly the way a Simm was supposed to be.

I thanked him for the meal. He bowed, painfully no doubt, and backed out of the room.

"Please inform Hassim Dupré that we will be returning to our own ship this morning."

The Simm bowed again, then shuffled off down the corridor.

It was time we called Lynch's bluff. Either we were still free citizens as he insisted or we were being held prisoner.

Sheba and I waited the better part of an hour for a reply. It finally arrived via the same servant who had conveyed my message to Dupré in the first place.

"His Excellency, Hassim Dupré has asked me," he signed with his thin wrinkled human hands, "to convey his regrets at your intentions to depart. A ship will be ready within the hour. He asks that you stop by his quarters before you leave."

Dupré was waiting for us, looking as cordial and diplomatic as ever.

"I trust your brief visit with us has not been unpleasant?"

"Not if we disregard the medical procedure we were asked

to undergo last night."

He pretended to look mystified. "Medical procedure?" He glanced at an aide who was seated nearby. The aide whispered something in his ear. Dupré frowned and nodded.

"Yes," he said gravely, "this bout of space fever is causing some concern. I'm happy to hear that you both were properly immunized. I should never forgive myself if we had allowed you to return to your ship carrying a potential epidemic with you unawares."

He nodded at the aide. The man got up and walked over to the controls of a console holovision. He made some adjustments, then waited for Dupré to speak again.

"The President, as I'm sure you realize by now, is keenly interested in reaching an amicable agreement with the ships of your fleet. I say this despite his little outburst when he was aboard the Ark. Our nerves have become a bit frayed since the last inventory of our solid reserves were made a couple weeks ago. I'm sure you've encountered the same reaction yourselves.

"Nevertheless, there are elements within our fleet who feel that President Lynch has been far too lenient in his dealings with you. None of these people are in this area of this ship at the present, I hasten to add, lest you think that you might be in any danger."

We nodded our appreciation with the false sincerity he deserved. He didn't seem to take offense.

"Last night some of these dissidents decided to take matters into their own hands. But," he said, nodding at his assistant to proceed at the holovision controls, "a picture will demonstrate better than any words of my own."

The aide flipped on the set. Some blurry figures began to take shape on the stage in front of the control panel. They were larger than the holovision figures most of us were used to, but this was after all the Number Two man's personal set.

When the images finally jelled we could make out a group

of men and women standing together. It only became apparent a few seconds later that the reason they were standing so close together was because their hands were tied behind their backs with a common cord. There were about twenty or twenty-five of them in all.

"These are hostages recently taken by some radicals. Unfortunately, we have been unsuccessful thus far in convincing them that this sort of behavior is not in the best interests of the Confederacy."

"You mean they're refusing to obey the President's direct order?"

Dupré sighed. "I'm afraid there's no more delicate way to put it. That is precisely what they seem to be doing."

"Why?" Sheba said.

As happens in space when communications are subject to all kinds of unexpected and sometimes novel radiation, the figures tended to pass in and out of focus, occasionally breaking into electronic squiggles. I began wondering how much of this interference was accidental and how much was induced just so we couldn't get a clear look at any of the so-called hostages.

"The dissidents are demanding three things: First, that your fleet inform the President or his representatives of your ultimate destination. Next, that you agree to cooperate in farming the belt of asteroids we are coming up on. And, finally, that you take an oath of allegiance to the President and the NWC."

"Is that all?" Sheba asked.

"Yes, madam," Dupré replied. "That is all."

So, this was to be their next move. They couldn't get the information they wanted out of us chemically, so blackmail was the final alternative. Only, I didn't believe for a moment that the figures represented by the hologram were really hostages. I believed they were Lynch's loyal toadies, play-acting for the sake of this last non-violent gambit.

"If you have any doubts as to the authentic identity of the

hostages," Dupré said as if reading my thoughts, "I have here a list of names and addresses—former addresses, of course. If you would like to peruse them…."

He handed us each a copy of the list of hostages.

Of course, I didn't expect to learn very much from such a list. Even if the names were legitimate, how did that prove they were really being held against their will?

"All of the names on this list were under suspicion prior to the evacuation. Some were actually under confinement of one kind or another. They were taken with us by Presidential order for humane reasons."

As soon as I heard him use the word "humane," I was ready to dismiss the entire business as a hoax, when my eye was caught by a name in the second column: "Ena, AKA Sissy. Address unknown."

My heart began pounding as I searched the hologram, trying to distinguish the faces there.

"Would you like to see a close-up of anyone in particular?" Dupré asked innocently.

"This one," I said. "Ena-Sissy."

"Certainly."

He motioned to his aide. A moment later the image of a young woman appeared on the projection stage. It was still a poor quality transmission. Even so, the expression on her face, the alternating looks of fearful little girl and proud woman, convinced me. It was Sissy all right.

Chapter Thirteen

There was still the possibility that the image had been made on Earth. All the so-called hostages, including Sissy, might already have perished far away in the final cataclysm. There was only one way of knowing for sure. I asked Dupré for a personal interview—or at least an individual holocast. He agreed to ask the dissidents to grant my request.

It would have made things easier if the hostages actually were a fraud. In that case, Lynch would have no sword to hang over our heads if we refused to accede to his demands—short of atomizing us. But I was almost ashamed to realize, as Dupré's assistant requested that "Miss Ena-Sissy" be brought to the holovision center, that I was willing to sacrifice the entire fleet's security for an assurance that Sissy was alive and well.

A few minutes later Dupré's aide received word that the HV center was ready for transmission. Dupré gave the go-ahead, and a moment later the image of my dear friend from Alpha-II began to materialize on the holovision stage.

"Sissy," I said. "Is it really you?"

The small figure glanced about, looking for the source of my voice. The niceties of holocasts and hyperphotic space travel were still beyond this final refugee of the great Civil War. Just two months ago she was eating half-cooked tree toads and sleeping under leaves. The only society she knew was a tribe of child-like people who, by a freak chance, had survived the massive irradiation of that planet. When I found her she had a vocabulary of less than a hundred words. Despite her keen natural intelligence, it was still a long way from that primitive existence to the storybook gadgets of 23rd-century technology.

"Where are you, Wah-wah?" she said, calling me by the name she had known me by on Alpha-II. She looked even more frightened than she had seemed in the group hologram.

"I'm here in the ship with you. We'll be together again—soon. Be patient."

She stared in confusion at the camera. To her still half-childish mind a disembodied voice made no sense.

Then the image abruptly dissolved.

It was almost too much to hope for. After weeks of poring over ship's lists and personal messages posted by the fleet's passengers in hopes of finding the names of relatives and other loved ones, I had come to resign myself to my loss of Sissy. Now, suddenly, I had her back again.

My excitement must have been obvious during the trip back to the Ark, because after a few minutes into the flight I realized that Sheba was watching me curiously.

"You love that girl, don't you?" she said.

"Yes," I said, only then realizing for the first time the truth of my own feelings, "I do."

Back on the Ark, though, my exuberance gave way to a more sober mood as I considered the predicament we still were in.

"Lynch has got us right where he wants us," Boston said in the conference room where Mneh and the rest of the leadership had gathered. "He must have planned it this way all along. I'll give him that much—he prepares for any contingency."

"You don't buy the idea that a group of dissidents took some of our people hostage without his orders?" I said.

"Do you?"

"No. There's no logical reason for their being on his ship in the first place if they weren't brought along for just this purpose.

It's Lynch's own idea, all right. But what are we going to do about it?"

I looked around the table. Mneh stared back at me through watery eyes. He had listened in grave silence to the report of our visit to Lynch's flagship. The old Simm looked weary. Perhaps, I thought, the strain was beginning to take its toll.

"One thing is clear," he signed slowly. "Lynch needs to mine that belt of asteroids, and he needs our help to do it. No doubt he figured on a shorter trip than we did, though I doubt that he had less time to prepare than we did, no matter what he says. My guess is that he believed all along what he was told about the supernova."

"Then why did he deny it? Why did he throw everyone who did believe it into jail?" Sheba said.

"To avoid a panic," her husband replied. "He must have decided early on that a general evacuation of the solar system wasn't feasible, or that something on that scale just didn't suit his purposes. So he convinced everyone—almost everyone—that there was nothing to worry about, while at the same time constructing a fleet to evacuate his chosen few when the time came. I'll bet that ship of his is chock full of corporate chairmen and generals."

It was hard to believe that even a man as ruthless as Marshall Lynch would sacrifice an entire solar system for his own selfish designs. But then I recalled the cruelty he had practiced during the Civil War, the stories that never found their way into the news or the official histories but traveled instead by word of mouth with a relentless insistence: extermination camps on Uranus under the guise of medical quarantine; mass castration of the supporters of the United Worlds revolt; and, of course, the intense and illegal radiation of the planets in the Centaurian system, which I had firsthand knowledge of.

"I don't see where we have any alternative," Boston said. "If we don't cooperate with him, he'll blow us out of the sky."

"And if we do," I said, "he'll take control of our fleet."

Boston regarded me with surprise. It was the first time I had challenged him. Mneh took note of this fact as well. The note of dissension seemed to revive him.

"You are both right," he signed. "But I don't believe Lynch can't farm the asteroids without our help. It would simply take him longer to do so on his own. And it would mean his possibly losing track of us in the meantime, which he has no intention of doing. "

"I agree," Sheba said. "As I see it, there's only one thing for us to do: Free the hostages."

"You're not serious," one of Mneh's assistants objected. "Those ships are a fortress. Why, we don't even have a decent laser canon."

"True enough," Sheba said. "We'll just have to capture some of Lynch's own weapons."

Boston glanced around the table with an incredulous smile. Then he turned toward his wife. "Have you gone crazy, Sheba? Why, Lynch can pick us off like flies anytime he has a mind to. We could never get close enough even to see their weapons, let alone capture any of them."

"We certainly can," she replied with the same confidence that was beginning to make some of us believe—or at least want to believe—that she was onto something. "Walter and I were close enough to do it just a few hours ago. We can get close enough again. Only this time we'll be prepared."

"How could we pull it off?" I said. "And what's to stop Lynch from doing us all in even if we succeeded?"

"We'll make Lynch our prisoner, our counter-hostage, if you like. If his fleet fires on ours, Lynch dies."

Mneh moved his head slowly from side to side and moaned the way I had heard Simms do when they were sick or dying. "Vengeance is mine, sayeth the Lord," he signed.

"It's not vengeance we're after," Sheba said. "We want those hostages. And we want to get free of Lynch. If we don't, he'll plague us for the rest of our lives. Didn't those Israelites of yours ever take up arms? Didn't their deity ever urge them to defend themselves?"

The old Simm shook his head some more and signed, "Thou shalt not kill."

"Well?" I said. "Do we put our heads together and see what we can come up with? Boston?"

He looked toward Mneh, then regarded Sheba as if she had just betrayed a closely-guarded family secret.

"I follow our leader Moses Mneh," he said.

Mneh seemed half asleep. I couldn't tell if he was ill or just feeling his years. I had never seen the effects of advanced age in a Simm before. On Earth they were always put to sleep before they reached that stage of their lives.

"Let's meet again in the morning," I suggested.

Afterward I asked Sheba, "What's wrong with Mneh?"

"Probably too much fasting. Boston told me he wouldn't touch food or water while we were away. He's hoping for another revelation, I suppose."

"Will Boston support him no matter what?"

"It looks that way, doesn't it?" Her black eyes were shining. Her forehead was creased. She took a deep breath. "I love the man. But his blind devotion to Mneh exasperates me. I can't understand what strange power Mneh has over him. I think he would follow that old Simm into the jaws of death—and take us all with him.

"It isn't easy having to go against the one you love. But if we leave it up to Boston and Mneh, Lynch will execute those hostages one by one just as sure as you and I are sitting here, Walt. And I for one am not willing to give up my freedom again, even to save my neck."

"I agree," I said, rather more quickly than I had expected to. After all, just a few months ago I was a loyal citizen of the

New Worlds Confederacy.

We presented our plan to the leadership the next morning. Officially, the council now consisted of ten members: Mneh, Boston, myself and Sheba, as well as two of Mneh's assistants and four members of the ship drawn at random without regard to their human or Simminoid parentage. Sheba made the presentation. At first it drew less than an enthusiastic response. But when she pointed out that she and myself would bear primary responsibility for the mission and that we would require no more than two others to accompany us, interest began to grow. In the final vote, Mneh, Boston and Mneh's assistants voted against the proposal. The rest of us voted in favor.

We were counting on Lynch's notorious vanity. We had never actually laid eyes on him during our recent visit to his fleetship. All our contacts had been with Dupré, his second-in-command. This time we hoped the big man himself would meet with us, since we intended to make it look as though we were about to concede to his demands. The trick would be to isolate him, then take him hostage and so force the release of the people he was holding.

Nothing to it!—except that Lynch was protected by the crack Presidential Guard while we had little more than our wits to work with. Still, the consensus was that, even if we failed, the worst that could happen was enforced servitude, which was all we had to look forward to anyway if we met Lynch's demands without a fight. The real trick would be to get away from Lynch's warships after the hostages were safely aboard our own vessel. We assumed that, with the President in our custody, his henchmen might not be so ready to open fire if the consequence of their action was to spend the rest of their days drifting aimlessly in space.

A gunsmith prepared two small antimatter weapons we could easily conceal on our persons and which wouldn't show up on Lynch's detectors. At noon a transmission arrive, advising us that the so-called dissidents were threatening to kill the hostages by day's end if we did not agree to help the war fleet farm the asteroids we were fast approaching. I dictated a conciliatory response, requesting another meeting aboard Lynch's fleetship. The reply stated that a vehicle would be by within the hour to pick us up.

I felt a good deal less cocky as I strapped on my antimatter gun than I did during the council debate earlier that day. For the first time, I had a chance to reflect on what I had gotten myself into. Had I made a mistake in hooking up with this band of mavericks and renegade Simms? But then I thought about Sissy. Even if I only stood to gain a few moments having her in my arms again, it would all be worth it.

Chapter Fourteen

We were passing through a star cluster. I had never been inside one before, though I had viewed several from a distance. From afar it looked like a solid ball of light. But as we approached, the ball disintegrated into thousands of individual stars. As we passed the outlying ones, I was reminded of the beginning of a snowfall when the first flakes float quietly by. Soon we were surrounded by stars. Because of their huge size, some looked deceptively nearby. The sky became bright with light. It was like having a full moon shining all around.

The view was almost enough to distract me from the real purpose of our mission. Even the space sled's pilot took time to gaze at the starry spectacle. It must have had a strong effect, because soon I noticed her popping a mood stabilizer. Ecstasy was a frightening experience to someone who had never allowed herself a good belly laugh.

We were accorded full honors, making me feel like a defeated head of state, which was probably the way Lynch saw us. At least we weren't searched. Dupré reassured us that the dissidents were certain to be "cooperative" when they learned that we had come to strike a bargain. We nodded frequently and let him feed and water us with a delicatessen of treats.

"I'm confident that an accord mutually satisfactory to all parties can be achieved," Dupré declared. We drank to that. Then we were invited to follow him to the ship's comm center, where I had been allowed earlier to see a holocast of Sissy. There were cameras already set up in the area where the hostages were being held, so it was just a matter of flicking a switch to transfer their three-dimensional images onto the HV stage.

It looked more like a scene out of an Old Order history text than something one would expect to find in the twenty-third century. The images of perhaps two dozen people appeared, all bound hand and foot. Some were gagged. They were lying on the floor of what appeared to be a storage hold.

"As you can see," Dupré said, "these people mean business. I hope you will believe me when I say that it pains me as much to show you these images as I am sure it must distress you to view them."

I nodded again, inwardly enraged at the man's cold duplicity. I didn't for a moment doubt where Dupré's "dissidents" were getting their orders. But we weren't there to prove Hassim Dupré a liar. We had come to free the hostages.

"What happens next?" Sheba asked.

A crease appeared in Dupré's brow. Such direct speech must have sounded to his ear as harsh as an obscenity.

"I will try to put you in contact with the leaders of the group, a man and a woman named Glick and Mogambo."

His aide made some adjustments on the HV console. The images of the hostages dissolved and a moment later those of a young man and woman appeared. The man seemed scarcely into his twenties, and despite the long hair he had grown for his role as terrorist, political ambition was written all over his face. He was probably one of Lynch's pets. His companion was a female copy. She was wearing a crimson tunic, to indicate her radical politics, I supposed.

"This is Mr. Glick and Ms. Mogambo," Dupré said, as if we were guests as a cocktail party. "Mr. Centaurus, Ms. Sheba and Mr. Mitchell." Dupré nodded to me. "You may proceed."

Before either I or Sheba could say anything the woman called Mogambo said, "We have been waiting for you. So have your friends. Are you willing to meet our demands and help us farm the next belt of asteroids we come upon?"

"We are," I said. "If you will agree to free the hostages and allow them to come back to Ark with us."

She glanced at her companion. They were no doubt under strict orders about what they could and could not agree to. "How do we know you will keep your part of the bargain?"

"You have our word," Sheba said, "and a few gunboats, I believe, to keep us to it."

Dupré smiled appreciatively at her sarcasm. But the young radicals looked worried.

"You would not be much good to us dead," Ms. Mogambo replied.

"We agree. So, why don't we stop nitpicking and get on with it. You've got what you want. We have no choice but to do things your way. Meanwhile," Sheba said, "innocent people are lying bound and gagged. At least have the decency to remove their bonds while we discuss the details of their transfer to our ships."

The pair conferred inaudibly for a few moments. Then Glick said, "Every effort is being made to see that your people are made as comfortable as possible. We are not going to be rushed into anything."

"I would hardly describe their present circumstances as comfortable," I put in.

"We would like to meet in person with you and with President Lynch," Sheba said, "to work out the details of the hostages' release and to discuss plans for the mining expedition."

It was the first time we had mentioned Lynch. It was diplomatic of Sheba to call him by his former title. But the mention of Lynch's name threw our interlocutors into confusion. We waited while they conferred again. I felt sure they would have loved to drop this play-acting and turn the matter over to Dupré.

"We cannot speak for President Lynch," they replied eventually.

"All right," I said, "then suppose you tell us how you propose to release those hostages to us. Are they free to leave right now? Can we assume that Lynch will back up any agreement you make about them?"

"We speak for ourselves—the League for the Preservation of the NWC. We recognize Marshall Lynch as our President, but any actions we take we do so on our own. We can negotiate for the release of the hostages, but we cannot speak for what is to become of them after that."

We turned to Hassim Dupré.

"Mr. Dupré, can we assume that the hostages are free to leave this ship once the dissidents release them?"

For once, he looked ill-at-ease. "Of course, any such contingencies would have to be referred directly to the President."

"May we have the opportunity, then, to meet with Mr. Lynch to iron out these details?"

Dupré bowed graciously.

"I will certainly refer your request to his attention."

Lynch was more than willing to meet with us, although you might not have guessed it from Dupré's circumspect version of his reply: "The President has asked me to convey his invitation for an interview following the midday meal." Lynch's eagerness was understandable. Unlike our own trim, ray-powered ships, his war fleet required vast amounts of light elements to keep them moving. Although much of this fuel was renewable, some was inevitably lost in the process of energy conversion. At the speeds we were traveling and the amount of time we had been in flight, those big energy guzzlers were by now running dangerously low.

We dined on earthly treats. Mitchell, the third member of our delegation, was amazed at the variety of the delicacies provided. There were even vintage wines, among them a Pouilly

Fuissé bottled in 2217. After the meal we were shown into a reception room, a more sumptuous version of the conference chamber on the Ark. Dupré told us Lynch would join us presently and invited us to turn on some music and make ourselves at home.

We had already agreed on a battle plan. If Lynch arrived alone we would simply draw our weapons and take him prisoner. If he was accompanied by one or more aides, I would deal with the aides while Sheba and Mitchell took care of Lynch. It wasn't a very elaborate plan, but none of us had any experience in this sort of thing.

Lynch came in with one of the military men that had accompanied him on his visit to the Ark. He was dressed in his uniform, festooned with all sorts of medals and decorations. I greeted him deferentially, then moved toward a sideboard where a bottle of wine had been chilling. That gave me the chance to get behind him. I reached into my tunic and, while pretending to be occupied at the sideboard, withdrew the weapon that had been pasted under my arm. Then I wheeled and pressed the gun against the general's ribcage.

"Don't move, Mr. President. You're being taken prisoner."

My turning from the sideboard was also the signal for Sheba and Mitchell to draw their own weapons so that they all would be taken prisoner simultaneously.

The aides immediately raised their hands over their heads. But Lynch's hands remained at his sides, and his jowly face wore a big grin.

"I'm afraid you're the one who has been taken prisoner, Mr. Centaurus," he said.

I thought he was only trying to divert my attention. But his grin continued to widen and Sheba, I noticed peripherally, looked worried.

"I think he's right, Walter," she said.

At that point I noticed the three armed figures facing me in the doorway. I still figured we had a stand-off at worst, until Lynch's fat body began to shake with silent mirth. Then I saw that the gun in Mitchell's hand was pointed not at Lynch but Sheba.

"Drop it, Walter," he said, "or I make a vacuum where Sheba's heart should be."

Chapter Fifteen

We were disarmed, shackled and led to detention cells by those same three armed men who had been standing by. I would have wrung Mitchell's neck if I had been able to get my hands on him. Had we been done in by one of Lynch's own people after an honest struggle, I might have accepted our failure as a brave plan gone awry. But knowing it was one of our own who had betrayed us, someone chosen at random—or so we had believed—was too much to bear.

We were placed in separate cells, bare boxes a few yards square and barely high enough to stand up in. The walls were soundproof, I learned when I tried to make contact with Sheba by rapping on them. I had little hope left of coming out of this venture alive. It seemed pitifully ironic that I had survived the destruction of the solar system, traveled untold light years into the heart of the galaxy, come within an ace of being reunited with the only woman I had ever loved, only to face death by a firing squad or its equivalent.

But I didn't have long to brood on these gloomy thoughts before Lynch's people came for me.

They took hold of my arms and hurled me out into the corridor. The shackles on my legs caused me to lose my balance and fall. But my captors took no notice of my bloodied nose as they lifted me up and dragged me down the corridor with them. They threw me into another cell, this one slightly larger than the first and induced a charged field across the entrance so that I could be seen without being able to escape: I tested the strength of the field and received a bad burn on my finger for my effort.

Shortly thereafter I received my first visitor, none other than my old friend, Hassim Dupré.

"I regret to find you in such reduced circumstances, Mr. Centaurus."

"I regret them myself," I said.

"Perhaps if you had not been so foolish as to make an attempt on the life of the President…."

"I made no attempt on his life. We were taking him hostage, just as your so-called dissidents took our own people hostage. The plan failed, that's all."

"But surely you did not believe you could get off this ship with the President as your hostage?"

"If it weren't for the traitor in our midst, we might have. Or would you have let us de-materialize your maximum leader rather than give up the hostages? Now that you have us, are you going to kill us now or later?"

Dupré raised his hands in a gesture of profound distaste. "Please, Mr. Centaurus, Let us not talk of such barbarisms. We have no intention of doing you any physical harm. In fact," he said, lowering his voice as if every word both of us said were not being monitored, "it is not unthinkable, despite the egregious crime you have perpetrated, that President Lynch might not find it in him to offer you an amnesty. Provided you cooperate, lend your good offices, so to speak, to the project which we spoke of previously."

"You mean the mining expedition?"

"Precisely."

"And if I refuse?"

"In that eventuality, Mr. Centaurus, you would place us in a most unfortunate position."

"You would kill me."

"Not necessarily," he said, still flinching at the directness of my speech. "You are more valuable to us alive then dead, whether you choose to cooperate or not. I'm sure that your comrades on the Ark will be of a more cooperative mind when they learn that your plan to capture our President has failed and that you will be enjoying our hospitality on a, shall we say, indefinite basis?"

"What about Sissy and the other hostages? What's to become of them?"

He shrugged. "I cannot speak for what their captors will do. But it seems reasonable to believe that, once the dissidents demands are met, the hostages could be set free."

"Can you get a firm commitment on that score?"

"Possibly."

"If the hostages are set free and transported to the Ark, you can hold me prisoner to make sure my people cooperate with your farming plan. I'll speak to Mneh and the leadership to persuade them. But if the hostages aren't released, the deal's off."

He thought about this for a few moments, then moved his head slowly from side to side. "I will see what I can do, Mr. Centaurus. But I make no promises."

"Remember, Dupré, it's a package deal. You do what you want with me, but the others have to go free."

It was only after he had left that I realized what I had done. How had I gotten the notion to play hero into my head? The idea was so out of character fort me, I began to wonder if what I had said to him hadn't in fact been programmed into my brain by my captors. How else could I explain his seeming compliance?

I was still musing on this possibility when a violent tremor shook my cell. It was followed shortly by another. Then the lights went out. I waited a few seconds and, when the lights stayed out, tested the force field across my cell. It was gone. I stepped cautiously out into the corridor. I could hear people shouting.

Some of it seemed nearby. I started down the corridor and abruptly bumped into something or someone.

"Is that you, Sheba?"

Our shackles had been removed when we were secured behind the force field, so now it was just a question of finding our way in the dark. By now I had a rough idea of the ship's layout, so I knew what I had to do if we were to escape with our skins intact.

Another tremor, even more violent than the first, shook the ship. We went tumbling over each other in the dark.

"I think I've sprained my ankle," Sheba said after I had helped her to her feet. I slipped my arm around her waist to support her.

"I'll only slow you down. You go on alone."

"We've come this far together. We'll get out of this together. Lean on me."

We made our way down the long, dark corridor. As we approached the aft of the ship a group of people brushed by us without seeming to realize they had done so.

"Why isn't there any auxiliary power?" Sheba asked.

"Whatever knocked out the main system must be affecting the backups as well. From the strength of those tremors, I'd say we ran into something pretty big."

"It must be some kind of energy field."

"What kind of field can disrupt a ship's entire system, including simple handlights?"

After innumerable false turns and more shin-barking than I care to remember, we reached what I believed to be the area where the hostages were being held. We could hear them calling for someone to let them out, like sailors trapped in the bowels of a sinking ship. In the dark, there was no way of knowing if anyone was still standing guard. I hoped there was, because without a voice key there would be no way of releasing them.

"Who's there?" someone called in the darkness outside the

detention chamber.

"The President has ordered that the hostages be brought to his quarters,

"What's the password?"

I sensed his body stiffening for action. This wasn't my line of work, but I managed to get hold of him from behind and exert pressure on his windpipe. He started to gag, and I realized that he wouldn't be able to speak into the voice-lock as long as I had his air supply cut off. So I switched to his arm

"Open up or I break it."

He cried out in pain. I let up a bit, but instead of cooperating, he called for help. I put more pressure on the arm, but the next moment I found myself on the floor, wondering if it was me or the ship that was spinning around so fast. Above me some sort of scuffle was going on. Then a body dropped to the floor beside me and I heard Sheba say, "It's no good, Walter. He won't give it up."

The lock, like the one in the mental hospital where I had been imprisoned, was set to react only to one particular voice. Unlike most of the rest of the ship, it did not require a central power source for its operation.

I tried my arm-bending routine again. He was no more cooperative now than he had been the first time.

"Listen, you damned fool," Sheba hissed in his ear. "This ship has hit an asteroid. Open that door or we'll all die right here in a few minutes when the walls start collapsing. You'll be floating in free space in another ten minutes."

Luckily the ship got the shakes again just at that moment. This time the tremor was so severe that all three of us went hurtling down the corridor. When it was over, though, the man was convinced. He spoke the magic word and the door lurched open, but only a few inches.

All three of us applied pressure to the door, helped from the inside by some of the hostages. The door yielded with agonizing slowness. Finally it was open wide enough for one person to slip through.

"Sissy?" I called as soon as I was halfway inside. Suddenly another body—warm, soft, and full of the natural fragrance of her womanhood—pressed itself against me.

"Walter," she cried, kissing my ear, my hair, my nose and finally my eager mouth.

Chapter Sixteen

In a personal sense, my mission was accomplished. The fact that Sissy and I, along with Sheba and the rest of the hostages, were still trapped inside Lynch's flagship floundering powerless in the void, seemed almost inconsequential. I was reunited with the woman I loved, the only woman I had ever really loved. But the ship continued to pitch and roll and every so often we heard commands shouted down the passageways. In the confusion Lynch's people seemed to have forgotten about the hostages. But I knew that sooner or later things would return to normal, the lights we go on again and we would be left prey once again to the President's thugs.

"We have to get out of here."

"Easier said than done," one of the hostages replied. He identified himself as an engineer who had been conscripted to help evacuate Lynch and his entourage from Earth. He had refused when he learned that the rest of humanity were to be left to perish. He was subsequently institutionalized but at the last minute was impressed into service aboard the war fleet. Even in my own Department of the Exterior, engineers had been in short supply for several years, thanks to a miscalculation on the part of the Department of Education. Along with the other hostages, he had been held in quarantine since liftoff.

The others all had similar stories to tell. Each had a particular skill that would be needed by a new space colony cut off from contact with its mother planet. The few who weren't technically skilled had been chosen for genetic reasons. Lynch had viewed the evacuation as an opportunity to begin the race all over again, this time basing it right from the start on conscious eugenic selection. Sissy, once a victim of the NWC's most pernicious weaponry, ironically was one of those selected for her superior genes.

The ship's landing docks were located on the port side, amidships. As best I could make out, we were presently located aft on the starboard side. An intricate security cordon kept unauthorized personnel away from the vessel's landing area. But the emergency which had thrown the rest of the ship into a panic might well have loosened security around the landing dock as well.

We filed out of the detention area single-file, keeping flush against the wall. Sheba led the way, holding my hand. I held Sissy's, and so on, so that we were all linked together like a chain in the darkness. We had traveled scarcely half the breadth of the ship when we began to hear voices. They were not the frantic shouts that had punctuated the darkness earlier. These were subdued and deliberate sounds, almost conversational.

Sheba and I went on ahead, cautioning the others to remain silent.

We were amidships at this point, on the lowest of the ship's three decks. The bridge was above us, two decks higher. The engine room was directly behind us. We proceeded cautiously, stopping every so often to listen. Eventually we drew close enough to make out an intelligible word or two. I heard a female voice say "magnetic response." Someone disagreed and said something about "premature degradation." It didn't make any sense to me, although I knew enough about a ship's systems to realize they were discussing the possible reasons for the power failure. Apparently we were near the auto-brain that plotted and executed the ship's flight through space. The voices were probably those of systems people responsible for maintaining the brain in good working order and making adjustments when it malfunctioned.

From the sound of things, they were as much in the dark about the power failure as we were in the impenetrable corridor.

We went back for the others and then managed to sneak by the systems people without drawing their attention. Now we were on the ship's port side. The next challenge we faced was to get up to the middle deck where the landing docks were located. With no light to see by and only the most rudimentary idea of the ship's layout, this seemed a daunting task. But one of the hostages was a ship designer. He had no firsthand knowledge of a major warship such as this one, but he had helped to design plenty of cargo vessels. Hopefully there would be more similarity than not.

According to him—his name was Riccardi—there should be an elevator at the end of the passageway. The device itself would, of course, not be working. But next to the elevator, for just such contingencies, there was supposed to be a hatchway and an emergency staircase. At least, that was how it was done on ships he had worked on.

He turned out to be right. Once we figured out how to open the hatchway, it was a breeze finding our way up to the middle deck.

We asked most of the hostages to stay back while Sheba, Sissy, Riccardi and myself ventured into the landing dock area. There was a murmur of protest from some of those left behind, but Riccardi's word seemed to carry considerable weight among them.

It was not entirely dark in the docks. Some starlight filtered down through the transom high above the pressure locks, enough for us to make out the vessels moored there. I counted a gunboat, a couple maintenance craft and three sleds like the one that had ferried us here from the Ark.

"There's at least one other set of docks on the starboard side," Riccardi whispered as we edged our way along the wall.

"What about security?"

"Hard to say. On a cargo vessel, security would be occupied with protecting cargo. But I'm sure there's a standing guard around these ships at all times."

I looked around but still saw no one.

"Can you fly one of those gunboats?" I said.

"I've never flown anything more complicated than a fixed-wing aircraft. Besides, there's no way to ignite its hydrogen cell without a power source."

"The space sleds don't require ignition," I said, having some firsthand knowledge of those vehicles from my work as Geo-Inspector. "Its brain would be shut down, but with any luck we could maneuver it manually and even tow the gunboat behind."

"You're not serious," Sheba said. "We couldn't outrun a kiddy car, flying magnetic with a tub like that in tow."

"We might get able to power up normally once we got beyond the ship's own field. Anyhow, what have we got to lose? Lynch can't pursue us until the main ship's power is restored.

"There's just one problem," I added. "How do we get the locks open?"

We looked up at the massive doors that separated us from the pressure lock and the void outside.

"There should be an emergency blow lock," Riccardi said. "A kind of compression device that explodes the door outward in a situation like this."

"Do you know how to activate it?"

"I can try."

Just then we heard footsteps approaching. It was almost impossible to conceal ourselves on the big open dock. We waited, flush against the wall, trying to stay out of the dim glow cast from the overhead transom. By the strengthening and lessening of that light I could tell that the ship was still pitching and yawing. I wondered how long it would be before its artificial gravity was affected.

Two uniformed figures advanced slowly across the docks. It

was hard to tell for sure in the gloom, but their uniforms did not appear to be those of ordinary soldiers. They were carrying what looked like briefcases.

"We're in luck," Riccardi whispered. Those guys are pilots. We may not have to blow the doors off after all. They can do it for us."

We waited until the two men separated, then followed one of them toward the big gunboat, crouching behind the sleds as we went. The pilot disconnected the hydrogen lines from dockside and pulled open the cockpit.

"How will he fire it without power?" I whispered.

"He probably doesn't realize yet that he can't."

The man—the other pilot seemed to be a woman—climbed into the cockpit. We heard the click of an ignition switch, but nothing happened. She tried again. Then we saw the cockpit open.

The other pilot was having the same difficulty. They conferred for a few minutes, then detached the lines connecting the smaller space sleds to the mother ship. It was time to make our move. Sneaking up behind the man, we overpowered him, then stashed him into the back of the sled. We waited until the second pilot was safe inside her own sled. Then I crawled back to the hatchway where Sissy and Sheba were waiting with the rest of the hostages.

They followed us back across the landing dock. A low, steady hum was coming from the sled the female pilot had occupied. Any second she would blow back the doors leading to the pressure lock. I hurried our people into the nearest gunboat, then set about securing it to the sled where Riccardi and the unconscious pilot were waiting. I had attached tow lines before this, but never to a military craft. Meanwhile, the other sled was firing. No doubt its pilot was wondering what was taking our own so long to ignite.

Finally I heard the same low, steady hum coming from the

ship we had commandeered. I hastily climbed aboard, having secured the hatches on the gunboat now safely in tow behind us. Just as I locked the canopy above my head, I heard an explosion. I looked up to see the heavy polysilicate doors fly suddenly forward from their moorings. The first sled began inching out into the pressure lock. We followed, hoping that the bulky gunboat behind us would not be visible until we were clear of the lock.

Once inside the outer lock we became weightless. I took over the controls from Riccardi, keeping the sled and its tow well behind the sled ahead of us. But I knew the pilot there had suspected something when we did not come up alongside as we approached the outer hatch. I could even see her head turn to see why I had not come up alongside according to normal operating procedure. Finally I saw her hand go up. I raised my own in reply, and suddenly the big outer hatch blew back just as the inner doors had

I was unprepared for the gloom that awaited us outside. We had spent so much time in the vicinity of bright stars that I had grown accustomed to their light. Normal space travel is a dark, lonely business, with only the anemic glow of very distant bodies to relieve its monotonous night. But this return to "normalcy" seemed even darker than I remembered it.

Mostly, though, I was preoccupied with navigating our way back to the Ark. I had a set of coordinates to work with, but they assumed that the Ark and Lynch's flagship had not varied their relative positions, something I could not count on, given the upheavals that had overtaken that flagship. I was hoping my sister pilot knew something I didn't, so I laid back, letting her lead the way. Once we had achieved cruising speed, the gunboat I had in tow presented no difficulties. But there was no telling what the pilot in the ship ahead would think once she saw that I had made off with one of the Confederacy's warships.

A few minutes out began to get some flickerings on my comm board. They were hardly reliable, given the power shortage, but some of the readings were troubling. Our coordinates made no sense. We couldn't possibly have traveled that far in just a few short hours, but the auto-brain calculated our speed as almost twice what it should have been.

I looked out at the seemingly fixed points of light, hung like dull jewels against the velvety black. Then I looked straight ahead. There seemed to be nothing there. If we were following the course of the Ark, where was the Ark itself headed? Absurd as the idea was, it was as if we had reached the end of the universe and were heading into infinite, empty space.

Riccardi agreed that the course we were following couldn't be right. Meanwhile, our flight speed continued to climb. I wondered if the other sled was getting the same readings, but I didn't want to risk making voice contact. There would be time enough to let her know our true identity after we had drawn closer to our destination.

The scanner finally showed a blip well to the starboard and almost twice as distant from Lynch's ship as the Ark should have been. There was nothing else on the screen, not even a space rock. I fixed on the blip and set a manual course for it. The ship ahead, after hesitating when she finally spotted the gunboat I had in tow, decided to follow. We flew peacefully enough until we reached retro. Then my sister ship suddenly crossed my bow at a dangerously close range, so near in fact that I could plainly make out the reflection on her tinted goggles.

She came around in a wide circle, then made another pass from the opposite direction, this time homing in on the gunboat behind us. The sleds were unarmed. The pilot of the other sled might be a devoted follower of Marshall Lynch, but she was no a kamikaze. Or was she? I wondered as she swung around for a third pass.

We continued playing space chicken all the way through the last stage of our approach to the Ark. Perhaps the pilot in the other sled imagined a gruesome death awaiting her and was bent on taking some kind of revenge before it happened. Whatever her motive, she was giving us a bad scare just as we were about to come home free.

Finally she lined herself up for a head-on collision. I zigged, then zagged, but it was no use. The gunboat we were towing made us much too cumbersome to match her own small vessel's maneuverability. On she came, her nose set directly on ours. We seemed seconds away from annihilation just when we were drawing so close to the Ark that I could make out her hull glowing like a dull ember ahead.

"She's going to ram!" Riccardi shouted.

The next thing I knew a fierce light filled the sky all around us. I figured I was on my way to eternity. I even thought I could feel the chill of the void penetrating my thin clothing. The ship rocked violently from side to side. When I opened my eyes the light was gone, not vanished, but swirling like snow. I had never seen light behave like that before. It didn't seem light at all but a cloud of fireflies all heading in the same direction. I searched the sky around us for some sign of the other space sled, but there was nothing. I turned to see if I still had the gunboat in tow. Someone in it raised a hand in the all-clear sign. I glanced down at the launchers below him. One of them was empty, a dark scorch where a missile had been fired.

Chapter Seventeen

It seemed like weeks instead of just hours since I had left the Ark. With no planet anymore to call home, the Ark had come to represent all the warm feelings I once associated with the word Earth. Now, as the lone material object in what was fast becoming an inky black void, that leaky old tub seemed even dearer to me.

Sheba and I were welcomed like the lost son and daughter we had almost become. The hostages were just as warmly received. We gave a brief account of Mitchell's betrayal and the power blackout aboard Lynch's fleetship that had allowed us to make good our escape. Then Mneh and Boston invited Sheba and myself into the conference room. Meanwhile, the hostages were brought below-decks for some food and fresh clothing.

The first thing I remarked was that the Ark seemed to be still enjoying full power.

"Actually, we're on a backup," Boston told me as I dug into a container of space rations. They never tasted better. "That's one advantage a ship like this has over a suped-up job like Lynch's. We're made for the long haul. We might be put together with spit and chewing gum, but you have to do more than knock out one system to put us permanently out of business."

I asked what was the cause for the power failure. Boston and Mneh exchanged troubled glances.

"It's still a bit early to say," Boston said. "Our systems people are going over every nut and bolt. It could be a differential in our magnetic generator. It could even be some kind of interstellar field."

I might have accepted either one of these explanations if it weren't for the queer looks the two of them continued to exchange.

"I hope you aren't keeping something from us," I said, glancing at Sheba, who seemed to share my concern. "If it's something serious I'd rather know now rather than later on. I think Sheba here agrees with me."

"She does," Sheba said for herself. "After all, it's hardly a coincidence that two ships flying as distant from each other as the Ark and Lynch's ship should be struck at the same time by the same problem."

Mneh and Boston stared back at us with grave expressions. Finally Mneh nodded, and Boston began to speak.

"You're right. It's foolish of us to keep anything from either of you. We'll be needing each other too much in the coming days. The truth is," he said, "we think we may be headed for a dead star—what they used to call a black hole."

You didn't have to be an astronomer to what this meant. Dead stars were the bane of every space traveler, the deadly icebergs of the twenty-third century.

"We still know very little about such objects," he said, "for obvious reasons. It's been almost impossible to study them without succumbing to their gravitational fields."

"How did we get caught up in this one?" Sheba asked.

"That star cluster we passed through when you set off for Lynch's ship played havoc with our auto-brains. By the time we set them to rights we had already entered the dead star's outer gravitational field."

"Good Lord."

"What do we do now?" Sheba said.

Boston took her hand. I knew that Sheba had earlier resented Boston's not asserting himself more, and now she gently but deliberately withdrew her hand from his own. Mneh reached across the table and gently joined their two hands together again.

"This is no time for dissension," he signed. "We have come this far, perhaps we shall even yet endure."

Sheba regarded him with a mixture of affection and exasperation. "How can we endure when we're headed straight into a black hole?"

"We know very little about dead stars," Mneh said, "that's true. But the more we know, the less certain we are that they mean certain death to anything that comes within their reach. It might be quite the contrary, as a matter of fact."

"What do you mean?" Boston said.

"Look at it this way. Physical matter, as we call it, takes on a different appearance—you might almost say a different reality—depending on the dimension in which we view it. Molecules seem solid enough. So did atoms, once. Then we learned that atoms were composed of particles, and particles were made out of even smaller particles, until finally we understood that matter and energy at the most basic level of existence are indistinguishable.

"We know now that this arrangement is also reversible. Most of our modern weapons are premised on this discovery. But antimatter is more than just a destructive force or a scientific plaything. It's a mirror reality of the one we live in. And it exists in huge quantities throughout the cosmos. How huge we still have no idea because it isn't measurable. In fact it isn't even visible, unless...."

"Dead stars?" I interrupted. "But I thought that theory was discounted a hundred years ago."

"It was. But, just as Newton's theories got a rebirth when we achieved interstellar capability, the old antimatter theory of black holes has come back into vogue."

"So you're saying they might be a kind of looking glass. Like the one in the story I was reading about a little girl who found a magic mirror she could walk through and enter into an entirely different reality."

"If you like."

"Or," Boston said, "they might very well in fact be very dense bodies which crush everything to an infinitesimal size, the way compactors crush old space ships for scrap."

Then Mneh spoke again.

"I'd like to add something else." His small black eyes took on a sparkle that I hadn't seen since our first weeks aboard the Ark. "Scientific speculation is all well and good. But if there's one thing I've learned since my initiation into the intellectual life of humans, it's that your theories have a way of going in and out of style, re-appearing several hundreds or even thousands of years later. For how many centuries after a Greek discovered the atomic theory was it discarded before the scientific community re-adopted it?

"The only things that remain constant are the ideas themselves. They persist through time and space. That's because they originate somewhere well below our conscious minds, expressed in art and religion as well as in science.

"So what? You say. Well, all I'm trying to point out is that we aren't the first group of people to go wandering in a desert. And we may not be the last."

Here was a queer combination of the old, rational Mneh and the religious fanatic he had turned into during our confrontation with Lynch's war fleet. I wasn't sure I followed his line of thought, but I felt nevertheless drawn to it.

There wasn't much in the way of preparations we could make for our entry into the unknown. It wasn't like entering a field storm, even though we battened down just as if that all that we were about to experience. We were told to expect turbulence and were already starting to feel some, but what we would eventually undergo had no correlative to anything a human—or any earthly creature—had ever experienced and lived to tell about it. Mneh thought that descriptions of ascensions into heaven, transfigurations and the like contained in his Bible might in fact be accounts of the sort of unearthly fate we ourselves were about to encounter. I could have backed him up his interpretation with some of my own readings—similar "supernatural" experiences described in Hindu and Greek mythology. But I didn't want to add fuel to his imaginative fire. I was not adverse to such notions, but the skeptic in me was too strong to accept them on someone else's say-so.

The next day we held a general meeting. Surprisingly, the announcement of our possible fate seemed to cause much less concern than I had anticipated. It almost seemed that after months of sailing aimlessly through the void, any destination was better than none at all. To be sure, there was bickering about whose fault it was that we might be flying into a dead star, but even that argument had a resigned tone to it. And the notion that we might be transformed into mirror images of ourselves in an entirely new, previously invisible universe, actually appealed to some people.

Increasingly strong tremors began rocking the ship in the days that followed. One "afternoon"—we no longer had even the artificial days and nights which used to give our lives some semblance of a normal time frame—I came upon Sheba on the observation deck. She was staring out the starboard window at the last vestiges of the star cluster that had thrown us off course in the first place. At this distance it looked like a very faint minor star. There was absolutely nothing else visible in the sky.

"It's like watching the candle of your life gradually burn out."

I put my hand on her shoulder.

"How's Sissy holding up?" she said.

"Pretty well. She survived two decades of abandonment on Alpha-II, a cosmic hurricane, hyperphotic space travel, imprisonment. She's made of stronger stuff than I am, I can tell you."

Sheba smiled and for a moment she was again the lovely woman I met in that underground safe house. But her black eyes went dull again when she looked back out the window at the fading light that was all that was left of our old world.

"I wish I could be more philosophical. But I still don't believe it had to end this way."

"Who says it's going to end?"

She turned from the window and confronted me with those angry dark eyes.

"I'm not a child, Walter. And I'm not afraid to die. But I don't especially like the idea of dying for the sake of someone else's stupidity. This didn't have to happen, and you know it. If my husband hadn't talked all of you into listening to that senile Simm, we wouldn't be in this mess."

She seemed about to cry but then raised her chin in a proud, almost regal expression. "I'd better get below decks," she said. "Some of my things aren't tied down yet."

I was left standing alone in the observation chamber. As I stared at the remnants of that distant star cluster, I suddenly felt like a fool for believing that anything more than certain death lay ahead. It was only wishful thinking that had made me believe in the preposterous possibility that Mneh and Boston were holding out to us. Perhaps they didn't even really believe it themselves.

A young Simm entered the observation chamber. I was in no mood to be sociable at that moment, but the Simm, one of Mneh's assistants, put a hand on my arm and signed, "Please come with me, Mr. Centaurus. Moses Mneh has taken ill."

Chapter Eighteen

As we were making our way down to Mneh's quarters, another tremor struck the ship. I careened into the wall, barking my shin. One of the Simms put an arm under my own and helped me the rest of the way.

I found Mneh in bed, propped up by several pillows, looking old and frail. He signed a greeting and invited me to sit down.

"As you can see," he said, "I'm somewhat indisposed.

"Temporarily."

He smiled knowingly. "For the time remaining. Which won't be very long.

"But I didn't ask you to come down here to commiserate. I'm about to leave you just when you are about to face your greatest ordeal—by 'you,' I mean of course all the creatures aboard the Ark."

He paused and with great difficulty drew a breath. I began to wonder why I was being accorded this private audience. What he had to say at a moment like this obviously concerned everyone on board the ship..

"We fear the known, however unpleasant, far less than we do the unknown. I sense that fear in the ship despite any sign of visible panic. But I also have confidence that a new and perhaps better world lies just ahead for you. I wish," he signed, his dark eyes filling with tears—the first time I had seen a Simminoid cry, "I wish I could accompany you to that new world. But," he said, "like the Moses of the Bible, I will be denied entrance into the Promised Land."

He had always had a flair for the melodramatic. But the sincerity of his feelings couldn't help but touch me. He had taken seriously his job as leader of the modern-day Israelites. He believed there was a destiny shaping our lives, a providence of some kind that had seen us safely away from the destruction of the supernova. Now he believed that destiny was leading us into a better life beyond the dead star.

It was a bit much for my skeptical nature. But I had to admit that his vision had helped sustain us through our journey. Come what may, Mneh had lived up to both of his names.

"I have only one thing more to say to you," he said. "Then I'll relieve you of an old Simminoid's final whims." (Like many Simms I had known, Mneh had a knack of knowing what you were thinking before you knew it yourself.) "Since I feel fairly confident that I won't be making the journey with you to the other side of the black hole, I think it's important that we decide who the next leader should be."

He paused and drew another, labored breath. His assistant offered him something to drink. He obliged, then lay back and regarded me with a mischievous eye.

"I'm not yet as senile as you might think I am. I don't mean you personally, Walter. I'm referring to the way everyone humored me when I was fasting in the desert. That required a lot of tolerance, and don't think I didn't appreciate it. Mind, I'm not making apology. What I discovered during that period gave my life and, I hope, the Ark's, a new focus. Until then we were just a bunch of refugees. Afterward, we gained a better sense of our mission. After all, apart from Lynch and his people, we are all that remains of solar creation. Surely, we didn't evolve and flourish for so many millions of years just to be squashed out like our brother ants?

"You're still young, Walter. As you grow older you'll feel the need for a greater sense of purpose."

"If I grow older," I couldn't help saying.

Mneh nodded. "I think you will," he signed. "I think you all will. And that is why I don't want to you go leaderless into the unknown. But I don't intend to designate anyone to replace me. After all, the Ark is a democracy. On the other hand, I can't hide the fact that I have strong feelings about just which way you should be headed. And I guess I'm enough of a politician, and enough of an old man, to want to voice my preference before I pass on."

Another tremor shook the ship, not as severe as the last, but enough to remind both of us that we didn't have forever to conclude this conversation.

"Walter, I want Sheba to take over the leadership."

To say that I was surprised is to understate my reaction. Sheba had made no secret of what she thought of Mneh's religious experiences or of his capacity to lead once he had espoused them. And she had been outspoken about her opinions at council meetings. Those opinions had almost—might still—cost her her marriage. I myself had been sympathetic to her point of view. But I also couldn't overlook the real service Mneh's leadership had provided us.

"She has a mind of her own," he said. "Strong convictions and the courage to see them through. I don't agree with all of them, as you well know. But none of those disagreements are fundamental. I'm not choosing her for her ideas but for her character. She'll make the best leader."

He paused to take another, this time painful breath. The strain of the interview was now becoming apparent. His brow was moist, and his eyes had become watery, this time from pain. "Please convey my wishes to the assembly when it meets," he signed weakly as another tremor shook the ship.

I took his hand, that human appendage grafted onto him in his youth when his own Simminoid hands had been unceremoniously lopped off. Then I embraced him, realizing it might be for the last time.

The ship continued to shudder as I made my way up to the bridge. I wondered if Sissy was all right. But the cosmos wasn't allowing much time for such concerns. I had all I could do to keep my balance. If our gravitron failed we'd all be floating about helplessly.

Boston was already on the bridge. I asked how the situation looked.

"See for yourself," he said, indicating the control console.

The readouts were not to be believed. Our speed was incalculable. Everything indicated that we were rapidly falling toward the body of huge mass. But there was nothing on the scope, not even an errant asteroid. I looked out the observation window. There was nothing there either. But it was a peculiar kind of nothing.

I have seen the void in many different parts of our galaxy. It always gave me a cold feeling in my gut. A vacuum is nature's first abomination. That is why she spends so much of her time trying to fill them. But the void we were flying into was of a different order than those patches of interstellar nothingness.

It was absolutely black. But "black" doesn't begin to describe the intensity of the absence of light or anything else. It was the blackness of a night where there has never been day. It was the darkness that preceded even the void itself.

Yet, all our instruments were telling us that the most solid piece of matter known to man lay directly in our path, pulling us irresistibly toward itself. I stared straight into the blackness, fascinated even as I felt my bowels trembling with fear. Then I said, "Mneh wants Sheba to take his place."

Boston turned toward me, seemed about to speak, then turned back to the console.

"At this velocity," he said, "we'll either break up in the next hour or enter that promised land that Mneh talks about."

It was the first time I had heard a note of skepticism from him. Sheba came back onto the bridge at that point, wearing a strange expression. Moses Mneh himself was brought up as well, almost too weak now even to sign.

"Have you told him?" he asked, meaning had I informed Boston that Sheba was his choice as ship's leader. I nodded. There was a tense moment, then Boston took his wife's hand. Under the charged circumstances, the gesture affected us all very deeply. Mneh managed to lift his arm and touch each of us in turn. Then his eyes widened as flashes of brilliant light filled the cabin. The Ark gave a violent shudder, then became perfectly still. Mneh closed his eyes, smiled peacefully and stopped breathing.

The flashes of light stopped, but the calm remained. But the view outside was no longer just the awful bleakness of before. Instead, it had taken on a shape, if empty space can be said to have a "shape." According to our instruments, we were still flying into a vortex, a vortex that was all form without matter.

We joined hands with each other and with Mneh, too terrified to say anything. I thought back to my days on Alpha-II, that jewel of the Centaurian system where I had found Sissy. My real life seemed to have begun there, some thirty years after my actual birth on Earth. It was there that I learned what it was to become a living, loving creature. Whatever happened now, I was grateful for those precious days.

Suddenly the bridge went dark and the gravitron failed. I felt myself begin to float upward. Still we held on to each other. The darkness seemed to fill not just the space around me but to seep into my brain as well. This was death, I thought. And yet I was still able to feel the touch of the others' hands inside my own. Was I still alive, or was there really a consciousness that persisted after physical life ended?

We seemed to float for hours, perhaps for days. I even seemed to sleep and then awake again. I even dreamed, dreams of childhood, dreams of Mneh and Sissy. Each time I awoke I knew the others were still there with me, but still no one spoke. Were they already dead? Would I be the last to die?

There are treatments for certain diseases that require that the patient be clinically paralyzed, alive only in the sense that his body continues to function under life-support systems without any aid from his brain. He remains insentient, cut off from his own flesh, and yet conscious. He may endure this for two days or two weeks, depending on the therapy. Those who have received such treatments often say that they can recall nothing between the time they first lose touch with their bodies until the moment that they are able to see, hear, touch and move again. They are the lucky ones. The rest go insane—the mind's way of compensating.

I have always dreaded contracting a disease that requires such a cure. And yet, that was very much the state in which I seemed to find myself, suspended somewhere between life and death. I waited for insanity, but that too never came. Nor did I feel any panic. I seemed to have a limitless reserve of patience. If necessary, I could wait forever.

At some point a notion entered the void that was now indistinguishable from my own mind. It started as a simple idea, almost an abstraction: What if there were a single point of light? What if the void were no longer all-consuming?

I considered the possibility in a leisurely fashion, for how long is impossible to say—an hour, an eon? I pondered it until the thought gradually stopped being just an idea and started to become reality. At that point my notion, my whim, had become, I knew, inevitable. There was only one more thing to do: Open my eyes.

When I did I saw a brilliant, young star, more beautiful than any I had ever before seen. I felt a gush of pride in what I had accomplished. And, like Jehovah, I saw that it was good.

Then I woke the others to show them the brand new universe I had made.